BATTLE AT BEGGAR'S GULCH

Jernigan was already lighting the fuse of a second stick of dynamite. He raised up to toss the explosive just as a rifle cracked from the cahpel. The slug missed hitting Jernigan seriously, but it grazed his arm enough to throw off his aim. The stick landed almost under the two huge log doors of the front wall of the enclosure, the fuse fizzling. Then a tremendous blast rendered the door into splinters.

There came a loud yell from the rear of the enclosure, and Matt jerked his head around to discern its origin. It was the white-haired man, astride a large stallion he had taken from the stable in the midst of the confusion of battle. He ran it full speed for the blasted-away doors, then out into the open prairie. He moved so swiftly and unexpectedly that no one even tried to get off a shot at him.

As Matt watched the man disappear he hoped that Melissa had obeyed his instructions and was now safely above on the canyon rim. If not, the mysterious rider might well find her—and then. . .

Other *Leisure* books by Cameron Judd:

BAD NIGHT AT DRY CREEK
CORRIGAN
THE TREASURE OF JERICHO MOUNTAIN

CAMERON JUDD

BEGGAR'S GULCH

LEISURE BOOKS   NEW YORK CITY

LEISURE BOOKS ®

April 2004

Published by special arrangement with Golden West Literary Agency.

Dorchester Publishing Co., Inc.
200 Madison Avenue
New York, NY 10016

ISBN 0-8439-5284-9

The name "Leisure Books" and the stylized "L" with design are trademarks of Dorchester Publishing Co., Inc.

Printed in the United States of America.

Visit us on the web at www.dorchesterpub.com.

1

It was a strange trio of riders that met Matthias McAllison the day he drove the buckboard to Briar Creek.

Two of them were grizzled, dirty fellows, typical of the breed one might expect to encounter on the Kansas plains. They rode by Matt with no expression on their bearded faces and made no response to his greeting.

It was the other rider that looked so out of place beside the two saddle bums. He wore a black suit, a tie, shining black boots, and a stovepipe hat that in its day had possessed some degree of elegance. He was clean-shaven, and his long dark hair was wellgreased and combed back behind his ears.

He smiled at Matt as he passed and lifted the stovepipe hat slightly as he spoke his "good morning." There was a cultivated elegance to his voice, like a preacher. Matt figured maybe that's what he was, or perhaps an undertaker. But there was something about the bone-handled .44 strapped to his right leg which made that assessment seem rather doubtful.

Matt didn't waste his time contemplating the

5

three riders, though. He had an errand to do, and he could see the church steeple of Briar Creek growing ever nearer across the flat Kansas grassland. And the day was too beautiful, the sky too clear, and his spirits too high to let him think about any one thing very long. So after the riders had passed he threw back his battered hat, leaned back in the buckboard seat, and whistled an old fiddle tune to the sky.

He was a handsome youth, twenty years old, with curling dark hair and shoulders broad from work on the small wheat farm he ran with his father. The sun had tanned his face and lightened the ends of his hair, and his natural high spirits and vigor lent an appealing glow to his blue eyes.

His family had come from Kentucky, and the free spirit of the mountain man flowed in his veins. He was a hard-working youth and a priceless asset to his father, who knew full well he could never run the farm if Matt was not with him.

In fact, it was largely because he so needed the strong shoulders of his son that Porter McAllison had moved his family to Kansas. The year had been 1868, and the McAllisons had been barely winning the fight to keep food on the table back at their old homestead in Kentucky. Matt's rifle brought in plenty of wild meat, though, and the meager gleanings from the mountainside farm had provided enough for the family to get by.

But that was about all. After awhile just getting by causes a man to get restless, and in the case of the McAllisons, the restlessness had struck both father and son. It was a beautiful spring day that the family had packed their possessions into the buckboard and headed west on the first leg of a journey that they hoped would eventually take them to Colorado.

Porter McAllison had known that if he didn't go west his son would have gone alone—he would have had no other choice. The love of freedom was in him and the call of the west had reached him, and he could no more help heading westward than an eagle could help circling in the clouds.

So Porter had joined his son, taking his wife Rachel with him. It was on the trip west through Missouri that she had first developed a cough, and by the time they reached the vicinity of Briar Creek in southeast Kansas she had been too sick to travel any farther. So that's where they stopped.

The drunken old doctor in Briar Creek had diagnosed her disease as tuberculosis. Porter and Matt did their best for the suffering and increasingly wasted woman, but it was no use. She died before they made it through their first winter on the small farm where they had settled.

It had been rough without his ma, but Matt had made it. He had realized that his father needed him more than ever now that she was gone, and he had vowed in his heart to stick with him no matter what.

That had been five years ago. It was 1873 now, and Matt and his father had managed to make the dusty little farm into a successful livelihood. They grew red turkey wheat and lived off the small garden in the back yard, the milk from their old Jersey cow, and the supplies that Matt brought in from his periodic trips to Briar Creek, four miles away.

There had been a day when Porter would have made these trips himself, but no more. He was no longer a popular man in Briar Creek, not since he had gone against Sam Haskell. The fat and pompous landowner and mayor of Briar Creek had cast a coveting eye on the small farm with its limited but fertile acreage, and he had asked, or rather demanded, that Porter McAllison sell it to him.

McAllison had refused, not rudely but firmly. He was a proud man, a product of the Kentucky mountains, and he planned to keep what was his. But in Briar Creek Sam Haskell was not a man to be refused, no matter how politely. He ran Briar Creek like a king, and though he already possessed countless acres of wheat, he longed to take the small McAllison farm just as a man might purchase a jewel of great beauty but no practical value.

It was soon after McAllison had refused to sell that he discovered his credit was no longer good at the Briar Creek General Mercantile Store. Former friends who had at one time or another benefited from Haskell's favor no longer spoke to him, and when he stopped occasionally at the saloon he usually had to drink alone.

It had been rough on Porter McAllison when he finally realized what Sam Haskell had done to him, and pretty soon he quit coming to town at all. Matt wasn't treated so poorly; it seemed that at least Haskell didn't hold the sins of the father against the son.

So for several months now it had been Matt that would hitch up the old team to the buckboard and head down the dusty four miles to Briar Creek. It pained him to see what the worry and pressure had done to his father—the lines on his brow and the circles under his eyes were deeper now—but Matt knew that his pa would hold out against Haskell as long as one ounce of his mountain-man determination remained.

And Matt was determined to hold out just as strongly as his father. So he made the supply runs to Briar Creek without complaining, even though it hurt him, and sometimes made him angry, to be forced to pay cash while other customers right beside him bought on credit. But such were the results of being on Sam Haskell's bad side.

But with the Kansas breeze blowing in his face, the sun on his shoulders and the huge white clouds sailing across the sky, Matt had no worries. Even the team seemed to be infected with the beauty and glory of the day, and they stepped with a liveliness they hadn't displayed in months.

There is something about the sky in Kansas on a clear summer day which seems more vast than a mind can take in all at once. Matt grinned as he viewed the waves which swept through the tall grass when the wind whipped across the flatlands. It reminded him of the ripples he had seen skirting across the Mississippi when the family crossed over into Missouri.

The land about him was flat at first glance, though to the west were low, rolling hills that extended in a line across the horizon. There was as gentle swell to the land between the McAllison farm and town, which caused everything but the church steeple to be invisible to a traveler until he crossed the crest of the swell about two miles from the town limits.

Matt's eyes took in the entire west side of the little town with one glance as he topped the crest of the swell. There was a peaceful look to the little

Kansas town that was apparent at even that distance, a look that spoke of tranquility and a simple, unhurried lifestyle. In spite of the hate he felt for the mayor and his cohorts, and in spite of the fact that Briar Creek was known all over Kansas as "Sam Haskell's town," Matt loved the community. After all, it was home, and the people there were his people, even if they were a bit unfriendly. As he approached he could sense the spirit of calm resting on the bare, weatherbeaten town.

That spirit was shattered as soon as Matt drove the wagon into the single dirt main street.

When something big, something unusual has happened in a small frontier town, a man can sense it immediately, just from the feel of the atmosphere. There was something in the air at Briar Creek; it was visible in the faces of the townspeople, the rowdy play of the small boys, the frantic barking of the dogs in the streets and alleys. Something was up for sure.

There was a crowd of folks gathered in front of the brick jailhouse on down the street, and more were headed that way. Out on the jailhouse porch Matt could see sheriff John Harper standing, waving his hand in the air as if he was getting ready to say something.

Matt pulled the buckboard into the alley beside the General Mercantile Store and climbed down in a hurry. He was aching to know what was causing such a stir, and he aimed to find out. He hitched the team to a post close enough to the water trough so they could drink, then headed out into the street.

He came up beside a skinny fellow with a game leg who was trying to keep up with the rest of the folks with little success. Matt slowed down to talk to him.

"What's going on here, mister? I just got into town so I don't know what the stir's about."

The skinny fellow grinned and looked satisfied the way folks who are about to share big news always do. He spit a wad of tobacco amber into the dust and spoke.

"I guess you ain't heard, have you boy? Sheriff's posse caught Will Monroe a few miles east of here yesterday mornin'. They brought him in just this mornin', and word just got out a few minutes ago. All these folks are hopin' to catch a glimpse of Monroe, I reckon."

Matt could have died where he stood. Will Monroe! The most notorious bank and stage robber ever to plague the Kansas flatlands, and the leader of one of the most vicious gangs in the west. Will Monroe—finally caught, and right here in Briar Creek!

"Mister, you're pullin' my leg," Matt said. "Ain't nobody even come close to capturin' Monroe before. How did they do it?"

The old fellow was really enjoying the attention. Matt could tell it made him feel important.

"Seems the sheriff got a tip yesterday that Monroe and his boys was plannin' to clean out the evenin' stage, so they just up and took all the passengers off and replaced 'em with deputies with scatterguns and pistols. The rest of the posse followed some ways off. Well, sure 'nough, about ten miles out, out comes Monroe and his men—three of 'em—from some roadside scrub. Just as soon as they showed themselves, out of the stage windows comes them scatterguns and blows the three gang members into eternity quicker'n you could spit. Monroe winged one of the deputies before the posse came over the hill and took 'im prisoner. Like I say, they just brought him in this mornin'."

By the time the old man had finished his narrative he and Matt were standing in the midst of the crowd at the jailhouse. The sheriff was talking, and Matt caught the tail-end of what he said.

". . .So that's how we caught Monroe, folks. Don't nobody fret none about the safety of your home and kin—he ain't gonna get out. I aim to see to that. Will Monroe is captured for the first time and the last time. In a week Judge Cyrus Jordan will be here and we can bring Monroe before the court. Once he's convicted, I guess you all know what will happen." The sheriff paused and looked out across the crowd of faces.

"We'll have us a hangin'!" said a voice from the rear.

"That's right, Charley—a hangin'," said the sheriff. "But it'll be a legal hangin', takin' place only after Monroe has been tried and convicted. I'm gonna say this once, and once only—there ain't gonna be no lynchin' as long as I'm sheriff. I've seen lynchin' in the eyes of some of you men this mornin', but I don't want to see it again, ever. Am I understood?"

There was only silence for a minute while the sheriff looked across the crowd with his eyes that could make a body shiver. Then somebody said, "I reckon we'll do what you say, sheriff."

Somehow Matt doubted that they would.

It was then that a fat man in a fancy brown suit stepped from the shadows on the porch behind the sheriff. It was Sam Haskell.

Even the sight of the pompous, greedy man made Matt want to spit in his face. As it was, though, all he could do was stand and look at him with a dark gleam of hatred in his eye. He thought of his father, broken and weary from the stress Haskell had put upon him, while Haskell himself stood beaming and happy in the town that he ran, the glow of health in his cheeks and the pride of self-worship in his eyes. It wasn't fair.

The fat mayor stepped to the front of the porch and hooked his thumbs into his vest pockets. Matt could tell from his posture and smile that he was about to make a speech.

"My friends, this is truly a great day for Briar Creek, a day that will put this town on the maps alongside the bigger cities of Kansas. We have had the honor of capturing the most vile bandit of this state, a man who has been the plague of the frontier for many years now. He is a man with no love of his fellow humans and with no regard for mercy. But now he is caught, and he will be brought to justice. Yes, friends, this is a day to remember, a day to cherish."

Matt couldn't stand it. He knew if he had to stand and listen to that fat hog grunt out a speech his temper would get the best of him. So he turned to leave. He loitered aimlessly for awhile at the other end of the street. Haskell's voice droned on in the background. There was no way to get his supplies right now; the store clerk had closed up shop to join the crowd at the jail. Matt watched the huge clouds float across the sky. There was nothing else to do.

It was then he noticed on the western horizon a faint curl of black smoke rising to the clouds. He looked at it blankly for a moment, then Sam

Haskell, Will Monroe, the crowd, and the supplies from the store were forgotten, and in their place came a horrible, gut-wrenching realization of what that curl of smoke meant.

The farm. The farm was burning. It had to be—there was nothing else in that direction for miles. It all came rushing into his mind with a sickening logic. The three riders—sent by Sam Haskell to the farm to burn it out. And what of his father? What might they have done to Porter McAllison?

Even as Matt ran toward the buckboard he knew his pa would never have let a man put a torch to his home so long as the ability to resist remained in him. But the farm was burning, so Porter McAllison must be. . .

Matt shut out the thought as his nervous fingers unhitched the team from the post and he jumped into the buckboard seat. He shook the reins with such fury that the old horses reared slightly before they bolted forward. He urged them onward with a shout so loud it diverted the attention of the crowd at the jail.

It caught the attention of Sam Haskell, too, who watched the youth steer the buckboard toward the edge of town in a cloud of dust. In the fat mayor's eyes was a strange light, and a smile played faintly on his lips, for he too knew what was meant by the rising band of smoke in the west.

2

Porter McAllison lay in agony, his blood draining out through the horrible shotgun wound in his right side. All around him was flame; the grass in which he lay was burning, tiny tongues of flame licking at him as he lay helpless.

The house was blazing, and so was the barn, and now the wheat was beginning to catch. Through blurred eyes he could see his Winchester about twenty feet in front of him on the ground. But it would be of no use to him now even if he could reach it; the stock was shattered and the barrel was bent.

And the trio that had shot him and set his farm aflame were gone. He was left to die, and the worst he had managed to give to any of them was a nick in the shoulder. He had fired only one shot at the murderous saddletramps. They had shot him before he could even speak to them—shot him like a dog or a rattler, then torched his home while he was forced to watch.

He knew where they had come from, and who had sent them. They were Sam Haskell's men, for he had seen the greasy-haired one in the black stovepipe hat alongside Haskell several times before. McAllison wished he could have put a bullet into the man's greasy head instead of into the other rascal's shoulder.

He knew he was dying. The pool of blood, ever-increasing beside him, was sufficient proof of that. But even without that evidence he could tell death was coming. He could feel it.

He thought of his son. Quietly he whispered a prayer of thanks that Matt had not been there, for had he been he would certainly have been killed. Even now perhaps he was not safe. But at least he wasn't lying beside his father in another pool of red blood, wounded or dead.

Though it bothered him greatly, Porter knew full well Matt would do his best to avenge his murder. If he lived until his son returned home he would try to dissuade him, but he knew the effort would be just as futile as it was sincere. Matt McAllison was a man, no longer a boy, and his man's sense of justice would cause him to seek out his father's killers, no matter what the risk to himself.

Porter McAllison knew that as surely as he knew he was dying.

He closed his eyes and tried not to think about the pain. He hoped Matt would return home before he passed out, but unless he noticed the smoke from the burning house and barn, he would probably take his time in town, and it might be afternoon before he returned.

And by that time McAllison would be dead. He closed his eyes again and though of Rachel. He was grateful she could not see what had happened to her husband—how such an honest, hard-working man had been gunned down by a trio of prairie

16

trash under the orders of a monster named Sam
Haskell.

ii

The old team was on the verge of collapse, their
backs and sides dripping with lather, when the
buckboard pulled up to a halt in front of the
burned-out shell of what had been a house and
barn. Matt McAllison descended slowly from his
seat, for his instincts told him haste was useless
now.

He saw the body of his father in the front yard,
the fingers charred from the burnt grass and the
ground around him clotted with dried blood. There
was no breath or movement. Matt's vision blurred
with tears as he walked over to where the body lay,
still and quiet. Matt knew his father was dead even
before he touched the cold, stiff hand.

He cried in earnest then, hot tears streaming
down his face and loud sobs coming from his lips.
They were cries of horror, of terror, sadness,
loneliness, and hate—hate for the men who had
done this to his father—hate for the man who had
hired them.

Matt couldn't tell how long he remained there in
the awful vigil beside the body of his father, but
when he finally arose the sun was moving toward
the west and buzzards circled above. He stood and
looked at them blankly, not even realizing that he
had mourned almost the entire afternoon. For the
first time in his life he felt completely alone.

There were no tears now. He had cried out his
pain, his frustration, his disgust, and his horror.
He had cried out everything but the bitter hatred

17

for Sam Haskell and the determination to make him pay for what he had done. He knew his father would have called him a fool for trying to get vengeance against trash like Haskell, but that didn't matter now. His father was murdered, and Matt knew what he was going to do—what he had to do, no matter what.

He walked slowly to the remains of the barn, seeking a shovel. All the tools were gone, burned to ashes and blackened metal by the fire. But in the manure heap beside the barn he found what he sought. He took it, went back to where his mother was buried in the back yard, and beside it dug a resting place for his father.

It was almost dark when he completed filling the grave. He fashioned a crude marker from boards left from the burned-out house, and on it etched his father's name. He planted the marker in the soft earth mounded above the grave, then stood in silence for a long time, his hat in his hands.

It was totally dark when Matt finally left his parents' graveside. He looked across the yard to the only remaining building on the farm besides the tiny outhouse in the back yard. It was the little tool shed in which Porter McAllison had stored just about everything that wasn't good enough to use but which was too good to throw away.

"Porter, I swear you must be half pack-rat," Matt's mother used to say. Matt had often smiled at those words. He couldn't smile tonight.

He strode across the yard under the light of the stars which were just becoming visible over the horizon. He knew the shed contained just what he needed.

He opened the door and looked inside, blinking

until his eyes grew accustomed to the increased darkness. On the left-hand side of the tool shed, which seemed to contain everything imaginable but tools, was a large stack of burlap sacks which had laid there for at least three years now. Matt dug into them, moving them aside until he located what he was looking for—a shallow oaken box about a foot long. He picked it up and carried it outside.

The starlight was even brighter now and increasing steadily. When he opened the lid of the box, it gleamed upon the barrel of a .44 Colt revolver, cleaned, oiled, and brand new.

Matt's father never knew he possessed such a weapon. If he had he would have disciplined his son sternly, for a Kansas farm boy had no money to waste on a weapon he didn't need.

But now Matt did need the gun, for he had a man to hunt, and after he had found him, a man to kill. So it was with a sense of dreadful purpose that he dug a large handful of cartridges out of the box and dropped them into his vest pocket. He loaded five others into the revolver's cylinder before thrusting the gun into his belt.

The team was still hitched to the buckboard, but now that they were grazed and rested they didn't appear nearly so tired. Matt patted the nose of each horse before unhitching the team from the wagon. He led the youngest horse, a roan, across to the shed. He stepped inside and returned a moment later with an old saddle which had been retired years ago when the family still lived in Kentucky, but which for some sentimental reason had been brought along to Kansas.

He threw a blanket over the roan's back and saddled him, pulling the girth tight. He bridled the

horse, soothing it with soft words and gentle pats, **then** mounted.

"Old boy, I know you've traveled this road twice already today," he said to the horse. "But I want you to do it once more. I've got something I have to do." The words rang dead and cold in the night air.

He nudged the horse with his heels and headed away from the farm, sensing in his heart he would probably never return. He no longer could think of himself as a youth. He was a man, and the task before him was one only a man could handle.

He moved slowly through the darkness toward Briar Creek. There was no haste, no sense of hurry. He could afford to be patient, for he knew that when he reached his destination his prey would still be there. And Matt knew that he would find him.

3

Sam Haskell sat in his usual chair in the Red Deuce Saloon, as haughty as a king upon his throne. And truly that's what he was—the ruler of Briar Creek and all that lay around it. He puffed his expensive cigar and smiled a bloated, satisfied smile at all the merriment around him.

He had good reason to feel satisfied. The unexpected good fortune of capturing Will Monroe was bound to increase his prestige in the eyes of those high in the political ranks of Kansas. His brain reeled with visions of glory. He was the man who ran the town where Will Monroe would be tried and hanged, and that was one hanging that would draw folks from as far away as Dodge, Haskell figured.

He gave no thought to the murder of Porter McAllison—no more thought than any other man would give to squashing an ant beneath his foot. For that was all McAllison had been to Haskell—a pesky, bothersome ant that had committed the unforgiveable sin of refusing to give Haskell what he wanted. So Haskell had crushed out his life. After that, he was worthy of no more consideration.

Of course, there was still the boy to be dealt

with. Had things gone according to Haskell's original plan he would have been killed along with his father. But he had been present in town at the time, and so had escaped death. But he was just a lad in Haskell's view, barely past his teens—an even smaller ant to be crushed out should he become bothersome. But most likely he would be gone, scared away by the sight of his dead father and the fear that a similar fate might befall him. No, Haskell told himself, there was no reason to worry about the boy.

And anyway, tonight was not a night for concern but for jubilation. There was much cause for rejoicing in the capture of Monroe, and that was just what the townsfolk of Briar Creek were doing. All around the saloon men were drinking, talking, and flirting lewdly with the saloon girls. Beer and whiskey flowed freely and music sparkled from the piano in the corner. It was a merry scene to behold.

And over it all Haskell sat majestically, sure that nothing could shake his power, nothing could sway his will. In Briar Creek he was a god, and as Porter McAllison had been shown earlier that day, he was not a god to be mocked.

Haskell sipped his whiskey slowly. His eyes turned to the door as a lanky figure in a black suit and tall hat entered. It was Marcus Leach, the man who acted as Haskell's chief protector and gunman. It was Leach that had blasted away the life of Porter McAllison that morning—all in a day's work.

His eyes darted across the crowded saloon until he saw Haskell. He began edging through the crowd of saloon patrons and barmaids as Haskell watched him over the rim of his shotglass. Somehow the fat man sensed he wasn't going to like what Leach had to say.

Standing in the doorway behind Leach were Pierce and Tubb, the other two hired guns that worked for Haskell. Tubb's arm was in a sling.

"Well, Leach, what can I do for you?" Haskell asked when Leach reached him.

Leach's voice was smooth and mellow as he removed his hat and responded, "Mr. Haskell, sir, I would like to discuss, shall we say, some matters of finance with you. It seems that certain members of our little group are not pleased with the risks involved in some of our recent jobs." Haskell glanced at Tubb, who still stood unsmiling in the doorway. He had expected something like this sooner or later.

Haskell took a slow sip from his whiskey and studied the man before him a long time before he spoke.

"In other words, you're no longer satisfied with your wages," he said at length. "I must say that I feel complaints are unjustified. I think that the pay you, as well as your two cronies over there, receive is more than sufficient. If Mr. Tubb is a bit upset because of that shot he took, then perhaps he should be reminded that all of you received a sizeable bonus for today's job. And in your line of work, certain risks are to be expected." His eyes dropped to the floor in a gesture of finality and he took another sip from his drink.

"I think we might be better off to discuss this further," Leach returned. "While I might be in total agreement with what you just said, our two friends over there in the doorway I'm sure feel otherwise. Perhaps we should go to your office and

23

have a private discussion." His smile was every bit as hypocritical as his smooth words.

Haskell sighed. "All right, Leach, if you want to discuss this in my office, then we will. But it will be me and you alone. I'll not be pressured by all three of you at once."

"That's an acceptable proposal," Leach returned, the smooth and deceptive smile still playing on his lips.

Haskell rose and walked with Leach to the door where Tubb and Pierce still stood. He pushed between them without a word and stepped out through the swinging doors into the darkness. The pair started to follow him and Leach, but he turned suddenly to face them.

"Mr. Leach and I have business to discuss—alone," he said coldly.

Pierce started to protest, but Leach raised his hand to stop him. "It's all right. Let me and Mr. Haskell handle this."

Tubb and Pierce glanced at each other, somewhat dissatisfied, but Pierce shrugged his shoulders slightly and the two turned back into the brightness of the saloon, leaving Haskell and Leach alone on the boardwalk. They headed across the street toward the stage office above which Haskell kept his office. They climbed silently up the stairs to the second-story room.

Neither noticed the roan horse and its rider which plodded slowly into the street from out of the darkness. And neither noticed the piercing gray eyes that took in the whole scene through the barred windows of a jail cell.

Haskell unlocked the door and stepped inside, followed by Leach. When he had lit the fancy coal

24

oil lamp on the table, he seated himself and turned to Leach. There was no longer any pretension of civility in his voice.

"Look here, Leach," he exploded. "I'm paying you more than you could get anywhere else in these parts, and I'm blasted if I intend to give you or your partners another cent! You're pushing your good standing with me a little too far this time! There's really no point in this discussion—I've made up my mind, and nothing you can do will change it."

Leach's smile grew colder, more threatening. "Nothing, Mr. Haskell?" There was a deathly sound to the words.

"That's right. It's only because I have no desire for the public to see dissension between us that I brought you up here. And now I'm telling you to leave. Hired guns are a dime a dozen—there's no reason I should keep you on if you aren't going to be satisfied with your pay. My use for you is over. You can ride out with your two friends."

There was a coldness, a hardness in the eyes of Leach that made him appear more demon than man as the flickering kerosene lamp lit his dark features. His face remained immobile, as if it were stone, and flame flickered its reflection in his eyes. Something in his steady gaze caused a spasm of sudden fear to grip Haskell, and he stood, his broad mouth opening slightly and his breath quickening.

"Haskell," Leach began in a voice like death speaking, "there's no man alive that can talk to me like that. No sir. No man."

Haskell began to realize with a growing tenseness the situation his angry words had placed him in.

25

Panic welled up in him suddenly, and he began to push away his chair. "Now, look here, Mr. Leach, perhaps I was a bit hasty. I had no intention of—"

The fat man never finished his sentence. Leach's bone-handled .44 whipped out of its holster like lightning and pumped three slugs into the gut of the frightened mayor, knocking him clear over the back of the chair and into the floor behind it. The gun had fired rapidly, its roar reverberating for a brief moment.

It was that echoing roar which caused Leach to not hear the office door open behind him. He dropped his gun to his side and looked for a brief instant at what he had done. A faint smile flashed across his face, and he turned to escape from the office and the incriminating body of the dead mayor.

He ran hard into a tall, straight figure standing in the open doorway. Strong hands pushed hard against his chest, knocking him to his back upon the floor. He cried out in surprise and shock, his pistol flying from his grip and clattering to the floor in the corner.

He looked up into the expressionless face of Matthias McAllison. The face bore no indication of emotion, but in the eyes burned a strange light that Leach had seen many times before. It was the light that shone in the eyes of desperate men, men who had lost their reason and were controlled only by blind passion and hate. Had Leach been able to see his own eyes only moments before, he would have seen the same fire burning in them.

Matt looked away from the fallen man toward the body of Haskell. It seemed to Leach as he watched Matt's face that a sad expression came briefly over it. But Matt's gaze didn't linger long on Haskell's body. It returned to Leach, boring into him like a dagger.

Matt gestured toward the gun in the corner. "Pick it up."

Leach knew then what Matt had in mind. From the tone of his voice he could tell that the young man was totally serious about it, too.

"Now look here, boy, it was Haskell over there that ordered your father's death. I tried to talk it out of him, but it was not use. One of the other fellow's killed him. I had nothin' to do with it."

"I said pick it up."

Leach stood slowly, his face twisting into an evil smile. He edged toward the corner like a great black cat, his hand already extended to pick up the gun. He knew that the shots of a moment before must surely have been heard in the crowded saloon across the street, and he knew it would only be moments before their place of origin was located and men came to investigate. He had to get rid of this boy in a hurry.

"Are you sure you can handle this?" Leach asked him. "You're not even wearing a gunbelt, and once I pick up this gun I'll be clear to blow out your brains. I'm giving you a chance to back out of this. There's no reason for you to wind up like your father."

His hand flashed to the .44 as Matt drew the Colt from his belt and fired two quick shots. The black-suited man jerked and fell on top of his gun just as Matt felt something strike his head from behind. Lightning flashed before his eyes and he fell senseless to the floor.

Behind him stood the sheriff, a pistol in his

hand. With him were Pierce and Tubb, while other men stood on the stairs and the street below, drawn by the sound of gunfire.

"What is it, sheriff?" a voice from the street asked.

The lawman slowly shook his head as he stared into the now-silent room.

"It looks like we've got ourselves a double murder," he answered.

From his cell window in the jail a little way down the street, the eyes of Will Monroe were still watching, piercing and sad in the darkness.

4

i

Matt awoke slowly, laying on his back on something hard. Above him was an expanse of gray which he couldn't identify. His vision blurred, cleared momentarily, then blurred again. His head ached, and he let out a low moan. A face appeared above him, vague and hazy to his foggy eyes. He squinted and forced his vision to clear. It was Sheriff Harper.

"Well, boy, I see you've finally decided to come back to us," Harper said. He wasn't smiling. Matt couldn't recall a time when he had ever seen Harper smile.

"Where am I?"

"Where do you think you are, McAllison? You've just killed two men. This is the jail, boy."

The horrible image of the events that had just transpired began to flit across Matt's memory now. He realized the sheriff must have pistol-whipped him into unconsciousness just after he had shot Leach. And now he was in a cell, on a hard cot, and the grayness above him was the slate ceiling of the jail. The misery inherent in his situation was apparent to him, but only on the borders of his consciousness. Somehow it couldn't sink in with full force—he had killed, and now he was caught.

Before he had come to Briar Creek on his mission of vengeance, he had not thought beyond the killing of San Haskell. That one purpose had loomed gigantic in his mind, blocking all other considerations. And even that purpose had been thwarted—thwarted by the gun of the greasy-haired killer who had taken Haskell's life moments before Matt would have done the same thing.

But wait! Harper had said that Matt had killed two men. Surely he was not to be blamed with the death of Haskell as well as that of Leach!

"Hold it, sheriff," Matt said, becoming suddenly more alert. "I'm not going to deny I shot Haskell's gunman—'cause I did shoot him, and I'm not ashamed of it—but I didn't kill Haskell. I swear it! He was already shot by his own gunman when I got in there."

The sheriff looked several long moments at the young man. "There's no reason for you to lie about it boy—do you think you'll get off any easier just because you convince folks you only killed one man? We both know you killed them both, and there's no reason for you to waste anybody's time with some fool story to try to make yourself look a little more innocent. But tell me, son, just one thing—why did you do it?"

Matt's eyes almost filled with tears, for into his mind came the picture of the burning farm, the three riders, the dead body of his father. He realized what might come of the vengeful deed he had committed—hanging—but as he thought of the dead form of his father, he knew that the deed was something he couldn't have helped doing. There was no point in regretting it now.

"Haskell's gunmen killed my father, sheriff. Killed him this morning, and burned down our farm. My pa's buried in the back yard, and the whole farm, wheat, barn, and all, is burned to the ground. If you con't believe it, check it yourself. You must have noticed the smoke risin' this mornin'.

"Sam Haskell ordered my pa's murder. You know as well as anybody the trouble Haskell and my pa had with each other. I came to town aimin' to kill Haskell, but like I said before, his own gunman beat me to it. I killed that gunman because I know he's one of the ones that killed pa. That's why I did it."

The sheriff looked at Matt with piercing eyes, and for a moment Matt detected something in his expression which made him think that just maybe he truly believed his story. But the hope was shattered by Harper's next words.

"Son, Sam Haskell was a big man in this town. This was his town, and everyone knows it. Now that you've killed him, there's no jury in this world, especially in Kansas, that'll believe your tale about your pa. Any boy that would kill two men wouldn't hesitate to kill his own father too. I figure the jury will probably see you as a boy that wasn't satisfied with the livin' you were makin' on that farm, so you killed your pa to get his cash. Then you came to town plannin' to clear out Haskell's safe. You were caught, though, and you killed two men tryin' to get away. That's the way it'll look to any jury, and to be honest with you, that's the way it looks to me."

Matt felt despair tie a knot in his stomach. He could see the whole thing clear now. The sheriff was right—Briar Creek was Sam Haskell's town, and apparently the sheriff was Sam Haskell's sheriff. He was just as much a puppet of the dead mayor as any official in the town government. Even after death Sam Haskell wielded a powerful influence.

The sheriff rose and left Matt's cell, locking the barred door behind him. He exited the cell area through the heavy oaken door which separated the prison from the front office. Matt was left alone.

"Well, boy, it looks like we've both got ourselves a wagon-load of trouble, don't it?"

The voice had come from across the narrow walkway that divided the cell area. Matt realized that he was not alone after all, and he turned and looked across at the speaker.

It was Will Monroe that looked back at him. In the awful happenings of the day, Matt had forgotten about the capture of the outlaw. This morning he would have been excited beyond speech to actually lay eyes on such a notorious criminal. Now it didn't seem to matter much.

"I've got nothin' to say to the likes of you," Matt responded, lying back on his cot. His head ached like pounding thunder.

Monroe laughed. "Well, boy, it seems to me you're in pretty much the same place I'm in. I heard what the sheriff said. You're in here for murder, and you know as well as I do we're both gonna hang. Seems to me that we're both cut out of the same material. There ain't no reason for you to be uppity with me."

Hanging—feeling life jerked away at the end of a stout rope. Matt had never thought what it would be like before. But he knew that Monroe was right. Haskell had been a big man in Briar Creek, and there was not any way that a person convicted of his murder, whether guilty or not, could receive any lesser sentence than hanging. Every moment the dreadful reality of the horrible spot he was in became apparent to Matt. This was no dream, though it was worse than any nightmare he could have imagined.

"Boy, you ain't very polite. It ain't gonna hurt you to talk to me. Looks to me like you could use a friend right now."

He was right. Never before had Matt needed a friend worse than right now. And after all, in the eyes of Briar Creek he was just as much a criminal as Will Monroe. It was all so hard to grasp.

"Sorry. I guess I got a lot on my mind right now. I didn't mean to offend you."

The playful, sarcastic look left Monroe's face, and he looked at Matt with an expression the young man couldn't interpret. More than anything else it seemed to be a look of pity, of understanding. Matt couldn't hold the outlaw's gaze.

"Son, I reckon I know what a rough spot you're in right now." He paused and added more quietly, "I seen what happened with you out there."

Matt looked in quick surprise at the outlaw. "You saw what happened? Then you know that I wasn't inside of Haskell's office when those first shots were fired!" He stopped, then added sadly, "I guess it don't matter, though. There won't be nothin' worse about hanging' for killin' two men than for killin' one."

"Son, I think you've just learned a lesson I learned a long time ago. When a bad man is in a place of power, there ain't no way to fight him," Monroe said. "I could swear up and down that I saw you and that you didn't kill the mayor, and you could dig up all the proof in the world that you were innocent, but it wouldn't make any difference. You're their pigeon now, and that sheriff aims to see you hang."

It was true, and Matt knew it. He shook his head slowly in a gesture of despair. "You know, I always thought of a lawman as being a good man, not one to do like Harper is doin'. I guess trash like Haskell just draws other trash to it. But like I say, it don't matter. I did kill the other man so I reckon I'll hang for that anyway. Now that my family's gone and there's nothin' left for me I guess it don't matter so much." Matt hung his head, fearing that tears might come.

Monroe rose from his cot and walked over to the door of his cell. "Son, let me tell you about a time when I was in pretty much the same spot as you. I was raised in Idaho, the son of a preacher, if you can believe that. I was kinda ornery, but I was no hellraiser. I married back in '47—the prettiest gal you ever saw, she was. I worked as a blacksmith, and everything was fine.

"It was about three years later that the local sheriff took a likin' to my woman. He trumped up a murder charge against me, and locked me away while he courted her. She fought him, couldn't stand the sight of him, but he threatened to kill me if she didn't do what he wanted. She gave in after that.

"I got out of jail one evenin'—knocked a deputy

34

cold with my boot when his back was turned. I couldn't locate that sheriff, then I found him in my house—with my wife. I blew his brains out on the spot. My lady took sick right after that, and God help me, I couldn't stay with her 'cause they were lookin' for me since I broke jail. I knew they figured I had killed the sheriff even though I had hid his body and they didn't have proof. So a widow lady down in the holler took care of my wife while I hid out. It was right after that she died.

"I felt like dyin' myself then, and in a way I guess I did. I ain't the man I was before that—and never will be again. Once you take that step of revenge you've started down a bad road. I don't care how justified you might be, neither. Once you kill a man, you hang, or else you run. That is, unless you're a man like that Haskell fellow they say you killed. Then you can get around the law. But not us. Not me or you."

Matt had to think of Monroe differently after that, for he could sense for the first time what it really meant to be a man like him, an outlaw. Never before had he conceived of a man outside the law as being other than the worst kind of scum, but suddenly he realized there were a lot of things that could start a man off on the wrong trail, things beyond his control.

Will Monroe had been pushed by corrupt men into the place he was now, and the same was true of Matt. Was this the way he was to end his life? Locked away in a stone-floored cell until the time came for him to climb the scaffold to die? Matthias McAllison—born in the Kentucky mountains, hanged an outlaw on the Kansas plains.

He felt a bond between himself and the gray-

35

haired prisoner across the walkway. Monroe was right—they were cut out from the same material. Not bad material, but material that had been spoiled by circumstances. Matt felt as if he should speak to his fellow prisoner, but somehow there were no appropriate words. So he lay down, stared at the ceiling, and thought of sleeping.

Sleep was elusive, though. Too much had happened, too much had been lost, and now it seemed rest was lost too.

It was still dark; Matt figured it was about three in the morning. The coal oil lamp on the wall above the oak door was still burning, dimly lighting the cells and making the blackness outside all the darker. Matt ached for sleep, but still it refused to come. When finally he gave up trying to drift off, he dropped into slumber just before dawn.

It seemed he had barely slept at all when a loud rattle woke him. It was the deptuy bringing in breakfast. It wasn't much, just a couple of sourdough biscuits, three strips of fatty bacon, and a battered tin cup of coffee that tasted more like dirty rainwater than anything else. But it was good in his empty stomach, and he ate and drank ravenously. When he was finished, he looked across at Monroe, who had already finished his meal and was reclining again on his bunk.

"Mornin', neighbor. By the way, I reckon you don't mind if I call you Matt. You're welcome to call me Will."

Matt managed to grin and speak with a good humor that he really didn't feel. He was ashamed of his unfriendliness toward his fellow prisoner the night before and he wanted to make up for it.

"Sure, Will," he said. "I feel like a man that's

been stomped by a stampeding cattle herd. This durn cot sleeps like a rock slab."

Monroe didn't answer immediately but only looked at the young man with an expression that told Matt that his next words would be worth hearing. "Don't you worry about that hard cot," he said quietly. "You won't spend another night there."

That was a comment to catch Matt's attention for sure. He looked inquisitively at Monroe. "What do you mean?"

Monroe drew closer to the edge of his cell, and Matt instinctively did the same. His voice had been quiet, but it grew even lower as he said, "Matt, did you notice how nervous the deputy was?"

"No."

"Well, if you had took a close look, you would have. And if you'll think for a minute, you'll see why. There's lynchin' fever in the air if ever I felt it, and believe me, I have. It was spreadin' yesterday when they brought me in, but now since the mayor and the other fellow are dead it'll be ten times worse."

Matt felt the hair on the back of his neck prickle. He recalled the sheriff's warning to the excited crowd the day before—there would be no hanging. And he also recalled the doubt he had felt that the crowd would heed the sheriff's words.

"No sir, Matt. Neither one of us will spend another night in this jail, if I've got my guess right. Before the sun rises tomorrow we'll be in one of two places—claimin' our eternal reward or runnin' for our lives across the prairie. I don't know about you, but I would prefer the latter."

Never had Matt been in fuller agreement with

anyone. He spoke in a nervous whisper.

"But how do you aim on gettin' loose? We can't just stroll out of here."

"Matt, when a man has a choice between hangin' or heavin' a forty-ton boulder across a river, he can heave a durn sight better than you might think. I've busted out before, I can bust out again. But I'll need your help. Are you with me?"

Matt was, without hesitation. So it was in the making of plans that the prisoners passed the day. Desperate plans they were, but plans full of hope, the only thing left to doomed men.

ii

Billy Lancaster was worried. Not since he had been deputized full-time three years earlier had he seen a situation so tense as this one. There was a general air of danger in the atmosphere, an edge that cut into his nerves like a sharp blade.

Billy knew that the men of Briar Creek had lynching on their minds. Too many men had passed the jailhouse today; too many significant, hurried glances had been aimed at the brick building. Briar Creek was generally a calm community, but the presence of Will Monroe had stirred up the aggressive sentiments that lay below the surface of each frontiersman's peaceful exterior. And the death of Sam Haskell had only enraged the seething town even more.

Something would happen—tonight. Billy sensed it instinctively. He wished that Harper would return to the office that Billy had been watching alone all day. He wanted to discuss the situation with him, to get some idea of how two men were

38

supposed to hold off an army of angry men all bent on hanging the pair locked away in the back cells.

When finally he heard Harper's footsteps on the porch, Billy felt relieved. He stood as the sheriff entered, removing his battered hat and throwing it onto a peg across the room.

"Well, Billy, how's our pair of friends been doin' today? They give you any trouble?"

"No sir. Everything's been quiet around here today. And to tell you the truth, Mr. Harper, I'm worried. Things have been a little too quiet, if you know what I mean."

Harper sat down behind his roll-top desk and propped his feet up in front of him. "No, Billy. I'm not sure what you mean."

Billy struggled for the right words. He didn't want to sound like a nervous schoolboy. "What I mean, Mr. Harper, is that I think there's gonna be a lynchin' attempt tonight. This town is just too stirred up right now. And to tell you the truth, I don't see how me and you are gonna hold off a crowd by ourselves. There'll be way too many for us."

Harper's expression was dull, unreadable. "Of course there'll be too many, Billy. This place will be run over for sure." His unconcerned tone mystified Billy.

"Then what are we supposed to do to stop 'em?"

Harper stretched and yawned. "Nothin'."

Billy was dumbfounded. "What?"

"You heard me, Billy. Nothin'." Harper sat up straight and put his feet back on the floor and spoke with more intensity. "I don't plan to die to save the lives of those two. You know they'll both hang anyway. The way I see it, the quicker the better. It'll just get 'em off our hands.''

The young deputy was completely taken aback by the sheriff's attitude. It was the last thing he would have expected. "But what about the speech you gave to the crowd yesterday? You said you'd have no lynchin' in this town as long as you—''

"I know what I said," snapped Harper. "That's what I was expected to say. That's how Mr. Haskell wanted it. But in case you haven't noticed, Haskell ain't around no more. Catch my drift?''

Billy's mind was in turmoil. Everything he felt was his duty as a lawman was being challenged. Instead of the strong, courageous man he had taken Harper for, he saw him now in his true form—a snivelling coward who cared only for his own safety and how well he pleased the man who pulled the strings, Sam Haskell. And now that Haskell was gone, Harper was in control of his own actions and his cowardly and selfish nature was coming through. Billy couldn't believe he had been deceived so long.

Harper apparently sensed Billy's feelings. He rose without taking his gaze off the young man.

"Billy, I'm goin' outside to wait on the porch. It's gettin' dark, and it won't be long before somethin' happens, if it's gonna happen tonight. I aim to sit out there and wait for 'em. I got no plans to stop 'em, but I don't plan to let 'em walk in here without a show of resistance. A man in my place has got to put up a good front. It's what's expected of me. But I don't want any interference from you, understand? You stay inside and guard the prisoners. But once that gang comes through the door, don't try to stop 'em. You'll just get yourself killed. You got that straight?"

"Yessir." It was a sullen response.

Harper opened the door, picking up his rifle where it leaned against the wall. He started to step out, but stopped suddenly and turned again to Billy.

"And one more thing, Billy—not one word of what I've said goes outside this room. Make sure you understand that."

"Yessir, Mr. Harper, I understand."

Harper stepped outside then, closing the door and leaving Billy alone with his thoughts—and turbulent thoughts they were.

5

It was a hushed crowd of men that gathered in the
livery stable on the north end of Briar Creek. And
it was a dark and frightful business they attended
to—the soaking of rags bound on poles in kerosene, the loading of rifles and handguns, and the
saddling of horses. But the nature of the gathering
was betrayed most obviously by the stout rope
coiled over the shoulder of one of the men and by
the sense of dreadful purpose which hovered like a
scent in the atmosphere.

There was a minimum of words, only the bustle
of men set on doing a cruel task. When they had lit
the torches and mounted the horses, the doors were
swung open and the processional slowly moved out
into the street.

Harper saw it from the front porch of the jail.
The torchlight flickered faintly down the dark
street. Billy Lancaster saw it too, and it put an end
to the turmoil in his brain.

He knew he had to move fast. He quickly rifled
through the top drawer of the sheriff's oak desk—
good! He had found the ring of keys. He slammed
the drawer shut and ran back to the door which led
to the rear section of the jail.

Inside, Matt and Monroe were tense, waiting on edge for the door to open. Through his cell window Monroe had seen the approaching riders, and both prisoners knew that even if their desperate plan succeeded their chance for survival was small. Matt wished that they had not waited so long to make their attempt, but there was no reason to worry about that now. He had feared the deputy or sheriff would not come back to the cell area before the vigilantes reached the jail. He was grateful to hear the creaking of the oak door.

Monroe's face looked livid in the coal oil light, and Matt could see every muscle in the outlaw's face tensed. Monroe stood where the door would hide him when it was fully swung open. It opened more quickly than Matt had expected, and the young deputy, apparently no older than Matt, stepped in. Matt could tell he was scared.

As the door shut behind the deputy, Monroe's hand shot out between the bars of his cell and grasped the young man. The deputy made a funny squawking sound as Monroe's strong fingers closed over his throat and pulled him up against the bars.

"Okay, son, let's have these cells open right now. We've got no time to waste. Open 'em or I'll choke you to death right here!" Monroe's voice was deadly serious. He lightened up his grip on the deputy's throat a little, though, so the young man could speak.

"Blast it," he gasped, "if you'd only waited a second before you grabbed me you would have seen that that's what I was goin' to do!"

Monroe looked so flabbergasted that another time Matt might have laughed. He let go of the

43

deputy before he thought better of it. "What?" The outlaw's voice betrayed his surprise.

Already the deputy was thrusting the brass key into the door of the cell. Incrédulous, Monroe and Matt could only watch him. What had possessed this young fellow to let out the very prisoners he was supposed to be guarding?

"I don't know if it's right for me to be doing this, but I sure know it ain't right to let no mob lynch a man, even if he is an outlaw or a killer. That's what I was told when I took this job, and that's what I believe." He swung open Monroe's cell door. "Ol' Harper might be intendin' to let you two hang without a trial, but I'll have no part of it."

"Well, I'll be. . ." Monroe's voice trailed off. He grabbed the keys from the deputy and quickly unlocked Matt's cell.

"Deputy, you don't know how obliged we are to you. But if you don't mind, I'll be needin' my gun."

"I can't give it to you."

Monroe wheeled around to face the trembling deputy. "Blame it, boy, I won't stand a chance—and neither will Matt here! If you let us out, at least give us a gun."

The deputy was firm. "I let you out, and there ain't no tellin' what they'll do to me 'cause I done it. But I ain't givin' you no guns. I'll draw the line there. You ain't gonna kill nobody with a gun I gave you. That vigilante gang is almost in front of the jail now—you'd best take off."

"How do we get outta here?" Monroe asked.

"There's a little storeroom off the side of the office. You can get out the window. But you'll

44

have to be real careful or they'll see you."

Matt had just opened his mouth to thank the deputy when Monroe's fist shot up lightning fast and belted the young lawman hard in the side of the face. He fell back against the wall, groaned, and slid to the floor unconscious.

Matt was aghast. "Why did you do that? He let us loose. Is that how you thank him?"

"Shut up, boy." Monroe shoved the deputy's limp body aside as he threw open the oak door again and moved quickly to the main office. The lights of the torches were visible through the drawn shades of the front window. The lynching party was directly outside.

Monroe grabbed two Winchesters from the gun rack behind the sheriff's desk. He tossed one to Matt, then dug in the drawer on the bottom of the rack for cartridges, which he stuffed in his pockets. He handed two huge handfuls of ammunition to Matt, too.

"Matt, there ain't no way I'm goin' outta here without a gun. And if you'll think for a minute you'll see that I done that boy an awful big favor. The way it looks now will make 'em think we bushwhacked him and got out ourselves. They'll go a lot easier on him now. Otherwise they might have hanged him."

Matt could see the logic in Monroe's action even as he belted on a .44 he found hanging in the corner. Monroe tore through the drawers of the sheriff's desk until he found his own pistol and belt where the sheriff had placed it the day before.

The sheriff's voice was audible right outside the window. Matt couldn't make out his words, but it was no matter—the vigilantes would be inside any moment. There was no time to lose.

Monroe threw open the storeroom door and headed for the window. It was a big room, apparently originally intended as a sleeping quarters for the sheriff or deputy. Monroe strained at the window; it was painted shut and refused to budge.

"Matt, get your tail over here and help me!"

Matt combined his strength with that of the gray-haired outlaw, straining with all he had in him. The window creaked, then slid open so suddenly that Matt almost fell through the alley. He caught himself, then glanced back toward the front of the jail. He could hear the sheriff still trying to talk down the mob, but other voices, loud and angry, were drowning him out.

Monroe thrust one denim-covered leg through the window, then pulled himself outside. He whispered urgently to Matt as the young man began to follow him out the window.

"Hug the wall, son. I can see the rumps of their horses right around the corner."

Matt was out in the alley now. He glanced toward the main street at the front end of the alley. Monroe was right—the tail-end of three or four horses was visible, the animals shifting restlessly as their impatient riders fidgeted in the saddle.

Monroe put a finger to his lips, then motioned toward the rear of the jail. Matt caught his meaning, and the pair began to edge toward the back of the brick structure. The noise in front was getting louder now, and Matt could sense that they had escaped just in time.

But they were still a long way from being safe.

46

Any minute now the sheriff would give up his pretense of resistance and the vigilantes would be in jail. Once they discovered their prey was gone, they would be all over town, scouring every corner and alley until they found them. Matt wondered where Monroe was leading him.

He ran smack into the outlaw's back as they rounded the rear of the jail. He had stopped without warning, and Matt's clumsy jostling almost made him fall. He said nothing, though, but pointed at the lightning rod which ran up the back of the building.

"We gotta climb—the roof's the only place they won't look right off."

Matt was incredulous. It seemed the last place they would want to be would be a place where they would be trapped, forced to cower like rats in a corner. He wanted to run, far and hard, and he started to protest, but the outlaw grabbed his shoulder gruffly and ordered, "Climb!"

Matt did as he was told, figuring that maybe it was best to trust the outlaw's intuition above his own. The iron was rough and cold in his hands, and it was hard to climb with any speed. He felt Monroe's hand against his rump, pushing him up. When his hands clasped the edge of the roof, Monroe put his hands under his heels and shoved Matt upward, helping him to roll onto the grimy black gravel of the roof.

Matt reached over the edge to grasp the older man's hand as he followed him up the lightning rod, breathing hard from exertion. Monroe pulled himself up beside Matt and the pair rested for a brief moment.

"Crawl over toward the front of the building,

but for land's sake don't make no noise and don't stick your head up over the edge where they can see you,'' Monroe whispered.

The pair edged quietly toward the front. The front wall of the jail extended up a foot and a half above the flat roof, making a kind of barrier that hid the pair from the men below. The glow of torchlight was visible to Matt above the top of the front wall, casting a weird glow into the sky.

Monroe lay down directly behind the high front wall on the gravelled roof. Matt did the same, and the two lay quietly, trying not to move or breathe too loudly. Matt noticed for the first time that he was soaked in sweat—cold, nervous sweat.

They could hear the voices from below.

''Men, I've told you that the prisoners will be given a fair trial. There's no point in hanging a man illegally when he'll hang legally soon enough.'' There was a murmur from the impatient and bloodthirsty crowd.

''Sheriff, we've made our demand. Give us the prisoners—now.'' Matt suspected from the tone of finality in the last word that the speaker had leveled a gun on the sheriff. There was a long pause.

''I hope you realize what you're doin','' the sheriff said with resignation in his voice.

There was a sudden bustle below as men dismounted, and Matt heard the sound of boots against the board porch. Hugged against the roof like he was, Matt could hear the men's progress as they moved quickly through the main office toward the rear of the building. He mentally predicted with absolute accuracy the cry that came up muffled through the roof: ''They're gone! They've jumped the deputy and got out!''

The street became a bedlam of shouting, running men, and the wild sound of spooked and rearing horses mixed with human voices. Matt knew that within a matter of moments a systematic search of every portion of town would begin.

He twisted his head to look at Monroe. The outlaw lay dead still, hardly breathing, it seemed. Right now the worst thing either of them could do would be to move, to make any noise at all that might indicate their hiding place. It made Matt itch all over to think about it, but he forced himself to stay motionless.

He couldn't help but wonder how they were going to escape Briar Creek now that they were out of the jail. They had no horses, and soon every man in town would be looking for them, if they weren't already. The vigilantes knew that the duo wouldn't have gone far in the short time—they had to be somewhere in town.

Matt figured there was nothing to do but trust his soul to God and his hide to Will Monroe. It was something vaguely like a comfort to have the man present. And in a way, Matt realized, he owed his life to the grizzled outlaw. If it hadn't been for his quick thinking, they both would probably be down on the street now, already captured and on the way to their own hanging.

It was a horrible feeling, knowing that all those men were determined to see them swing from a rafter or tree limb somewhere. For the life of him Matt couldn't picture himself as an outlaw, although he knew he had killed a man. For a couple of years now he had tried to think of himself as a man rather than a boy, but tonight on that jailhouse roof he couldn't think of a time he had felt more like a helpless child.

His thoughts were interrupted by a slight hiss from Monroe. He twisted his head to look at him, wondering if the outlaw had figured some way out of their predicament. It seemed to Matt like the only escape would be for them both to sprout wings and fly off into the night.

Monroe's whisper was so faint that Matt had to strain to hear it. "Next time you hear me hiss like that, move real slow and quiet toward the back of the jailhouse. We're gonna have to hope we can catch one or two of those riders off to themselves and surprise 'em. We got to get some horses if we aim to get outta here."

Matt nodded, then squeezed back down into his uncomfortable position again. Out of the corner of his eye he could see Monroe ever so slyly raise his head to peek for an instant into the street below, then drop back behind the wall again.

It seemed as if hours passed up there on the roof as Matt lay in the grime while the night breeze whipped his hair. He began to get anxious to hear Monroe's signal just so he could move. He couldn't hear anyone in the jailhouse now, but there was no way to be sure it was empty. Maybe the sheriff was down there, or some of the vigilantes. But when the time came to move, that was a risk they would have to take.

The street was almost empty now, the riders having moved farther and farther into the other portions of the town. But suddenly Matt heard the hoofbeats of a horse—no, two horses—moving down the street toward the jail.

"Let's take a look around back."

"All right."

The riders split up, one going down each alley on either side of the jail. Matt looked over at Monroe. The older man's face was twisted in steady, deep concentration as he listened to the sound of the horses' hooves in the dirt as the riders headed toward the back of the jail.

"I don't see nothin' around here."

"I guess they wouldn't hang around here anyway. But there's no sign of 'em anywhere else—by jiggers! You reckon they could be up on the roof?"

Matt's face froze into a stony scultpure of terror. Monroe hissed very faintly and motioned the frightened boy to crawl as they had planned toward the back of the jail. Matt didn't have to be told how important silence was right now.

"I'm climbin' up there to take a look," the voice said.

Matt began to sweat again in spite of the cool breeze. His left hand gripped the Winchester, and it was hard to crawl and keep it from rubbing noisily against the roof at the same time. The lightning rod was shaking already, indicating that the man below had already begun his ascent. Matt and Monroe crawled silently and as slowly, it seemed, as snails.

"Matt," came Monroe's voice in a quiet whisper, "when that feller's face comes up over the edge, I aim to kick in hard. I want you to jump the other man at the same time. It'll be risky but it's the only way. Got it?"

Matt's answer was a faint grunt. He was surprised at how little fear the prospect of jumping the rider brought to his mind. Maybe it was because he was full to the top with fright already,

51

and there just wasn't room for any more.

When Matt saw Monroe slowly rise to a stooped-over standing position, he did the same, gripping his rifle tightly and trying to keep his head low enough that the men below couldn't see it. A hand reached up over the edge of the roof, then another, and Matt knew a crucial moment had arrived—a life or death moment.

When the climber thrust his face up beside the lightning rod, he didn't even have time to focus his eyes before Monroe's heavy pointed boot caught him full force between his eyes, breaking his nose and catapulting him backward from the wall, sending him on a complete flip through the air before he landed like an overstuffed feed sack on the dirt, totally senseless.

And the still-mounted rider below could have sworn it was a wild renegade Indian that flew at him from the rooftop, eyes blazing and mouth wide open and the butt end of a rifle aimed right at his forehead. He dodged slightly, as much as he had time for, and managed to avoid having his head bashed by the gun stock, but the force hitting him felt like one of the Abilene cattle trains coming on full steam.

He was knocked clean off his horse, landing with a grunt on the ground with his attacker still on top of him. He tried to holler, but a strong hand calpped down vise-like on his throat, choking off his voice.

And the other hand, having dropped its rifle, pummelled his face like a hammer. His breath had been knocked out by the fall, and the choking grip at his throat was not letting him breathe at all. The constant pounding against his head was causing the world to go black around him. He knew he would be as senseless as his partner in a moment, so with his right hand he reached down to his belt, pulled out a hunting knife, and drove it hard into his attacker's side before he lapsed into unconsciousness.

Matt stifled a scream when the blade dug into his flesh, burning like a hot poker. He raised up and clamped his hand over the wound, watching the blood ooze through his fingers.

Monroe was beside him an instant later. "You hurt bad, boy? Stuff your handkerchief against that cut. We gotta ride outta here quick. You did right in not lettin' that feller yell—it would have been the end of us if he had. Now let's mount up on these horses."

It was all Matt could do to swing himself up on the dark stallion without hollering in pain, but he managed to make it. He took the reins in his left hand, then clamped his right over the bleeding stab wound in his side. He felt dizzy, but he urged his horse forward nonetheless, following Monroe and his mount out of the alley.

The outlaw paused at the end of the alley, looking in all directions before clicking his tongue and digging his heels into the sides of his black and galloping out into the deserted street. Off on the other end of town Matt could still hear the cries of the searching men.

It jolted pain all through him to sit astride the galloping horse, but he knew it was his only chance. The pair flew fast and silent toward the dark plains outside of town. The moon was obscured by clouds, immersing the prairie in a sea of blackness as thick as ink. It was into that sea of darkness that the duo rode as they left the town behind them.

We've done it, Matt thought, we've escaped from Briar Creek. It was impossible, but we've done it. But with every jolt of his stallion's hooves against the dirt, it felt as if that fellow was sticking the knife into him again and again.

He had escaped. But whether or not he had escaped with his life—well, that was another matter.

6

It was a cackling hen. It had to be—nothing else could make a noise like that.

Matt hovered in the limbo in which it seemed he had been for the past ten years. His mind wandered, floating free in space, not making any connection between events and memories, fantasy and reality. There seemed to be nothing at all in the universe except himself—and that noisy, cackling hen that punctuated his thoughts at irregular intervals with its jarring squawks. Where was it? The blasted thing was getting annoying.

Matt moved, determined to find the hen and make it stop its irritating cackling. A third thing suddenly entered his universe—a sharp pain in his left side that rendered him suddenly weak and drove him back toward unconsciousness again. Nothing made sense; he couldn't remember where he was nor where he had been, or even if it was night or day.

He struggled to open his eyes and failed. Then came the cackling sound again, louder this time, and more irritating. He tried to open his eyes again, this time succeeding. But the light struck his eyes like a hammer blow, and he squeezed them shut again. It was several moments before he reopened them, this time managing to keep them that way, mystified by what he saw.

Above him was a rough, unpainted board ceiling, and a similarly constructed wall ran down beside his right arm. He was laying on a straw tick, he guessed, judging from the prickly, scratchy sensation it caused on the back of his neck. Where was this place?

He twisted his neck to the left. Before him, across the small shed which to his eyes seemed somehow immense, sat two figures. One was Will Monroe, and the other was a small, bent man that Matt had never seen before. At the sight of Monroe, the memories of the escape began to return slowly, like the trickle of water in a drying stream. But still Matt couldn't place the other fellow, nor figure out where he had come from.

He looked old and shrivelled, his white hair long and uncombed, his beard full and reaching to his hollow chest. His cheeks, though covered with whiskers, looked sunken, and his eyes were set in two dark hollows. His eyebrows were thick and as white as his beard, and his skin was dark, wrinkled, and weatherbeaten.

The old man's clothes were ragged and dirty, and on his feet were crude moccasins, apparently hand-fashioned to cover his feet with no thought to appearance. They made his feet appear to be covered with leather sacks rather than any type of legitimate footwear.

The sound of that piercing cackle came again, and this time Matt determined its source. It was the old man, and the cackle was his version of a laugh. Apparently he and Monroe were absorbed in some humorous story or recollection, for both were talking and laughing loudly. Matt couldn't make out what they were saying due to the fog which seemed to hover around him.

The two men were seated around a roughly hewn table. They paid no heed to Matt. But when he moaned slightly, involuntarily, suddenly all their attention was focused on him. Monroe and the old man rose from the table so quickly that Monroe's chair tipped over behind him. They rushed over to Matt's bedside and knelt beside him.

"Matt, have you come around to us?" Monroe asked in a tense voice.

Matt looked at the outlaw's intent face and tried to speak. His throat was dry and he could hardly force his voice out.

"Will—where am I?" he asked, his voice cracking. Before the outlaw had a chance to answer, Matt added, "Could I have some water?"

The old white-bearded man moved with a quickness that seemed out of place in so ancient a character. He headed over to the opposite side of the shed, drawing a dipper of water from an old oaken bucket that sat atop a barrel in the corner. He held the dipper carefully to avoid spilling any of its contents as he came back over to Matt. Monroe lifted the young man's head from the pillow and cradled it while the older man touched the dipper of cold water to Matt's lips. The water was refreshing, almost immediately instilling the youth with a new strength and drawing him further out of his limbo and into the real world.

"It's good to see you stirring a little," Monroe

said. "I was really worried about you—afraid you might not make it. That was some bad knifing you took back there in Briar Creek."

"That's surely the truth, son," the old man interjected. "When ol' Will brought you in, you was in a bad way for certain. I was fearin' for your life. It's good to see you've rallied."

"Where am I?" Matt asked again.

"You're in old Jimmy's shed, Matt," Monroe answered. "You're safe here for the time bein'. We ain't too far from Briar Creek, but I don't think the posse will look around here for maybe a couple of days yet. Ol' Jimmy's shack is in a pretty remote place. Not many folks know it's here."

"I reckon that's right," said the old man. "I ain't got much use for folks comin' around much anyway. Unless, of course, it's an old friend like Will here." Then came the cackling laugh again, remarkably like the calling of an old hen.

Matt was thinking hard, trying to piece together the events of the recent past, and to place them in some sensible order. "What day is this, Will?" he asked. "How long has it been since we got away from the jail?"

"This is Wednesday afternoon. It was yesterday evenin' we got loose. We rode all night, or close to it, and you were in pretty rough shape the last half of the trip. Bouncin' around on that horse with that knife wound in your side didn't do you any good at all. I had to lash you onto the saddle toward the end to keep you from fallin' off. We made it to old Jimmy's shed here a little before dawn.

"I knew this place was our only hope. I had to get you to a place where you could rest, else you wouldn't make it for sure. Jimmy's lived out in these hills for years now, and I guess I've been one of his better friends over the years. He took us in, just like I figured he would, and he cleaned up your wound for you. You were out like midnight the whole time, and things looked pretty bad. These past few minutes is the only sign of life you've shown since we got here.''

"The posse—did it follow us?''

"Son, I've shook off more posses than an old hound has shook off fleas. I didn't take me long to lose 'em in the dark. I knew we would be clear just as soon as we got out of town. That wound of yours kinda interfered with my plan, but thanks to Jimmy here I believe we'll make it all right. What you need to do now is rest and try to get in shape to ride before the posse gets into these parts. They're figuring that we rode west, I'm sure. I cut south for the hills a little way out of Briar Creek though. That's when I lost 'em, and that's when you started fadin' out on me, too.''

Matt's thirst was gone now, replaced by hunger. The aroma of simmering meat reached him. He glanced in the direction of its origin, and noticed a black pot hanging above a fire in a roughly built fireplace at the end of the room. The smell was enticing, and his hunger must have shown in his face, because Jimmy hopped up from off his knee and scrounged up a pewter bowl and spoon, heaping the bowl full of steaming stew and bringing it to Matt. He poured the young man a large cup of strong black coffee to wash down the stew. Matt breached his thanks to the old man, then began devouring the food ravenously as Monroe continued his story.

59

"We've been tryin' to take care of you all day, or at least Jimmy has, because as soon as I got here I had to turn in, I was so exhausted. I just woke up myself a few minutes ago, a little bit before you came around. We've been talkin' about some of the times we used to have when we rode together before many settlers came to Kansas. It was rough times, for sure, but it was good times too. Lord, have we got some stories!" Monroe and Jimmy glanced at each other, and both laughed, Monroe in his deep chuckle and Jimmy with his high-pitched cackle.

Matt was slurping the stew noisily, not paying much attention to his manners. The food was delicious and invigorated him to an amazing degree, and he could feel the fog clearing from his mind. The wound in his side was noticeable, though, and pained him if he moved too suddenly.

"How soon do you figure the posse will be—did you say two days or so?"

"That's what I figure. They've got a lot of ground to cover toward the west before they convince themselves we didn't take off in that direction. But that don't leave you too much time to get back into ridin' shape." Monroe's expression became more serious.

Matt finished the stew and handed the bowl to Jimmy. He tried to move a little to see how well he could work the muscles in his injured side. It hurt, but he did better than he expected. Monroe placed his hand quickly on his shoulder.

"Don't do that," he said sharply. "You'll only make it worse."

Matt suspected that Monroe was not as optimistic as he had been trying to sound. He doubted that he would be in riding condition before the posse reached them.

"Will, there's no reason for you to stay here on my account. I ain't gonna get you caught just because I wasn't a good enough fighter to keep some man from stickin' me in the side. You go on. I'll stay.

"Matt!" Monroe's tone was stern.

"Yes?"

"You shut up. I'm stayin'." It was obvious from his tone and expression that further argument was useless.

So Matt lay back on his bed, letting his exhausted, wounded body rest in the hope that perhaps his wound would heal quicker than he expected. It was hard to feel optimistic.

It was just before noon two days later that Jimmy spotted riders approaching from the west. The posse had arrived.

7

i

Sheriff John Harper could see the smoke curling up from the chimney of the small wooden shack nestled among the low, rolling hills southwest of Briar Creek. Other than that there was no sign of life in the area. At first glance he might have thought the shack was deserted. But the rising smoke said it was not, so it merited a search by the posse even more than it would have otherwise.

Normally he would not have thought there was any possibility that the pair he was seeking would be holed up this close to Briar Creek, but one of the men who had been jumped behind the jail had said he had wounded one of them with his knife, and that just might have slowed their escape down considerably. Besides, it was obvious they were not on western flatlands; that area had been searched completely by the posse already.

So the little shed here in this remote region where so few people ever came was at least a possibility. Harper's blood raced as he lead his men in that direction. As he approached he drew his

Winchester from its case and held it before him on his big dun horse. There might be shooting— almost certainly if the pair were there. He didn't care if he took them alive or not; he just wanted them out of his way. They had caused enough interference in his life already.

There was no movement in or around the little shack as the band of riders approached. Harper studied the scene, then motioned for two of his burlier riders to dismount and approach the cabin while he and the rest of the posse stayed further back, their guns drawn and ready for battle.

The two men dismounted and scurried toward the little dwelling, their rifles gripped tightly and their heads held low to avoid being a good target should any sudden shooting from the windows begin. But nothing happened, and when the pair reached the little roofed porch of the shack, they flattened their backs against the wall on either side of the door. They paused a moment, then both moved together, spinning around and kicking in the door with their heavy-heeled boots.

A high scream from inside was their only welcome, and they trained their rifles at the source of the sound. It was a little scrawny man with a white beard and long hair, cowering like a kitten behind the table at which he had been eating his midday meal. His chair was overturned as evidence of the frightened haste with which he had arisen, and his bowl of soup was spilled all over the table as well as down the front of his faded flannel shirt.

"Wha—what do you want? Why are you bustin' in here like this?" The old man's voice was weak and trembling, apparent fear robbing his throat of any ability to speak above a whisper.

"Old man, have you seen a pair of drifters, one probably wounded, anywhere around here in the last two days? You'd best tell us straight."

The old man was breathing hard and shaking violently. "Lord, no, I ain't seen no one in I don't know how long," the old man responded, still hiding behind his table and staring at the rifles aimed in his general direction. "If I had, I swear I would tell you—I swear it!"

The pair looked at each other, mentally debating whether to accept the old man's story. There was something about the frightened sincerity of his voice and the honest look in his old eyes that made them tend to believe him. But it paid to make sure.

"You care if we take a look around?" The pair were already beginning their search before the words were out. It made no difference whether the old man cared or not.

The room was empty but for the table, two chairs, a barrel, and an old wooden water bucket. Next to the fireplace was a large stack of split wood, and an axe leaned against the wall. Against the side wall was an empty straw tick, and strewn about the room was every kind of trash imaginable. There was nothing else. In spite of the obvious barrenness of the room, the searchers checked every corner, as if they expected to find their prey hidden beneath an old rag somewhere on the floor.

Without a word of apology for their intrusion, the searchers finally stopped, warning the old man to keep his eyes open should any suspicious drifters turn up. They left abruptly, making a token effort to reclose the door whose latch they had kicked to pieces upon their entry. The old man watched silently. The pair mounted up with the rest of the posse, then as quickly as they had come they were gone.

The old man moved to the small window and opened the shutter slightly, watching the posse disappear over the low, sloping hill toward the east. The fear in his face was gone, replaced by a smile which said that he knew far more than he had just told. He laughed a strange, cackling laugh.

"You can come out now. It's clear."

The straw tick against the wall seemed to be alive as it thrust itself up into the air, scattering straw all over as it fell to the floor in a heap. On the rope slats which had held it lay Will Monroe and Matt McAllison, both laughing in triumph, the latter wincing in pain with every chuckle. They had split the bottom of the tick's cover, placing it over their bodies and working their way inside like human stuffing.

"I've never had so much trouble trying to not sneeze in my whole life!" Matt exclaimed. "That's a pretty clever trick, Jimmy."

"You don't stay alive out on the plains unless you know how to use your wits, son," the old man said, his eyes twinkling. He looked out the window again. "They won't be back—you can count on that. They'll never find your horses where I hid 'em. Right now they figure the only person in this shed is an old man whose probably still shakin' after they busted in on him like they did." He shook his head. "Blasted fools!"

Then he looked at the pair of straw-covered men in front of him. "You fellers may be pretty good at dodgin' posses, but I swear you're awful rough on straw ticks!"

It was about a week later that Matt's side was healed enough for him to be able to ride again. The parting with Jimmy was a sad one for him, for he knew he could never set foot in these parts again. The parting would be permanent. A strong bond develops between men who have faced danger together, and Matt discovered it was a bond that was hard to break.

But in this case it was necessary. Both Matt and Will had to go their way quickly, for the area would be crawling with lawmen and bounty hunters searching for them for weeks, maybe months, to come. Matt had no doubt that there was already a price on his head, and he had a sense of rather morbid curiosity to know how much it was. Perhaps that was knowledge he was better off without; he realized it might make sleeping difficult if he knew.

The sun was just rising over the eastern horizon as Matt and Will began their journey away from the rugged shed that had been their home for the last several days. Jimmy stood in front of the building, his face sad, and he waved at the departing riders as long as he could see them. And when the little bent man disappeared from Matt's sight, obscured by distance, the young man knew he had seen the last of him.

There was only silence as the pair rode through the morning side by side. Even when they stopped later on to eat a scant meal of the jerky which Jimmy had provided them, they said little. Matt was sad for two reasons: He found it hard to leave Jimmy, and he was bidding goodbye not only to

Briar Creek but also to everything his life had been up to that point. Kentucky, his mother, the Kansas farm, his father—all of it was gone now, gone forever. It was hard to believe, and hard to take.

Will Monroe was sad too, for he was aware of something that Matt had not yet realized. Soon the pair would have to split up, for riding together was far too dangerous to both of them. They could be too easily identified. And Monroe had grown to like, even love, the young man who had come into his life such a short time ago. A man always on the run finds few friends—Monroe realized that far better than most men—and now fate was to rob him of one of the most precious friendships he had ever developed. And once they were separated, the odds were much against them ever meeting again.

It was that night when Monroe explained it all to his young partner. Matt took it without words or any display of emotion. He slept little that night, though, and when the morning came his sadness had not dispersed.

The pair rode together for two more days before they split up. They shook hands and said little, then separated, Matt heading west and Monroe moving south. When Matt saw his friend move out of sight over a ridge, he felt very alone. It made the void left by the death of his father all the more tremendous and all the more painful.

And as Monroe rode off into the distance a nagging question kept popping up uninvited in Matt's mind: Whose bullet would it be that finally took the life of the outlaw? Living the life he did, Monroe could have little assurance that his life would continue, Matt realized. It made him feel sad to think about it.

It rained that night. Somehow it seemed appropriate.

Matt began drifting after that. He had no goal, no purpose—only endless days of wandering, constantly moving westward. His earlier dreams of life on the plains, the dreams that had kept him restless nights back in Kentucky, seemed like mocking memories now. Matt began to wonder if he would ever remember how to feel happiness again.

8

It was nighttime and the rain was falling in drenching sheets on the dirt streets of Wilson's Fork, Colorado. A lone rider, hunched over in the saddle, his hat leaking a steady stream of water in front and back, plodded slowly down the middle of the street, feeling every bit as weary, cold, and bone-tired as he looked.

It was Matt McAllison, known now to the world as Matt Stanton, a name taken to hide his true identity and to divert capture by any money-hungry bounty hunter or sheriff that might recognize him as the young farm boy wanted in Kansas for the murder of Sam Haskell. The previously clean-shaven face was now covered by rough beard, which further masked the identity of the young drifter who had wandered to Colorado with no specific aim except to escape Kansas and the stigma of being watched, and to leave behind the territory where so many bad memories were easily called to mind.

Matt's eyes were tired and bloodshot in the darkness as he scanned the bare street, the slow sound of his horse's hooves in the mud making a monotonous rhythm. There was no light except that which shone from a couple of shaded windows at the local hotel beside the stage office, and the brighter, more gaudy glow from the Silver Skillet just down the street.

He made his way in that direction after leaving his horse at the livery. He had only a few dollars in his pockets, the scant supply of money he had made from working at various odd jobs as he traveled west, scraping by as best he could. He loathed the idea of spending any of it, but his stomach was totally empty, and his head was swimming from lack of nourishment. Perhaps at the saloon he could find something to sustain him until morning. That is, if the saloon served anything more than liquor.

But an even more important possibility than food was the chance he could find work. He hoped that perhaps some of the personnel from some of the several large cattle ranches in the area would be there, and perhaps, if he played his hand well, he could pick up a job. If was either find work soon or starve. He was already well into autumn, and winter would come rapidly. Jobs were scarce, but he couldn't let himself give up hope—surely something would turn up sooner or later. He had told himself that many times, trying to encourage himself, but the words had rang rather hollow in his mind.

He was shivering from his wet clothing as he entered the door of the saloon. He removed his hat and shook it above the boardwalk before he was all the way through the door; he didn't want to stain the polished hardwood floor with rainwater.

The light, noise, and warmth inside were a

welcome contrast to the darkness and silence outside. It felt good to be around people again, even people he didn't know. It had been a long time, it seemed, since he had known a friend.

As he made his way through the crowd toward the bar, trying not to brush anyone with his drenched clothes, Matt thought of Will Monroe. Where was he tonight? There was no way to guess. The older man had given no indication of where he might go, and Matt suspected that Monroe himself had not known. Even if he had, he wouldn't have said. When a man is running from the law he doesn't give too many clues about his plans.

That was true for him, too, Matt realized. It was a strange feeling, knowing that he must remain at least partially an enigma to anyone he met, unable to share his true name and background because of the stigma which rested on him. He was every bit as much a man on the run as Will Monroe, though at least not as well-known.

"What'll it be?" The bartender didn't glance up as he asked the question.

"Got anything cooked up this time of night?"

The fat bartender looked up in disgust. Matt could tell he had no desire to cook this late in the evening with more people than he could handle pressing around the bar for liquor.

"Ain't got nothin' but some sourdough biscuits. They'll run you two bits."

"Got anything to go with 'em?"

"Sorghum, but it'll run you fifteen cents extra."

"I'll take it—and some coffee too." Matt fished in his pocket for change, wishing that he could afford something more substantial than sourdough biscuits and molasses. But a man can't be choosy

71

this late at night, he told himself.

The bartender moved slowly in getting Matt his supper, but eventually he laid the scant meal out before him, taking the change and dropping it into his pocket as he moved away. Matt began devouring the food, only then fully realizing how hungry he was. The meal seemed pitifully small, and he wished he could afford another helping. But his scarce funds made that an impossible luxury. He ate every crumb of his biscuits and mopped up each remaining drop of sorghum on his finger, licking it off. He was determined to get his money's worth.

His thorough cleaning of his plate did not escape the notice of the man standing beside him at the bar, for, as he drained his last drop of coffee, Matt heard the man laugh good-naturedly to himself before saying, "You must be right hungry, friend. Or else them's awful good biscuits."

Matt looked at the fellow, a bit unhinged by his friendliness. It wasn't something he was used to lately. He stared in surprise at the man, then realized with some embarrassment how ridiculous his ogling face must look.

"Yes sir, I reckon I was a bit hungry. I've been on the trail the last two months, and a good meal don't come along too often."

"If you ask me, it didn't come along tonight, either," laughed the stranger, glancing at the empty plate. He was a skinny fellow, as homely as he was thin, with deep wrinkles in his tanned face. His hair was thinning and brown, and he appeared to be in his mid-thirties, though his weatherbeaten features made it somehow hard to tell. His eyes twinkled, and Matt's instincts told him this was a good man, one he could trust.

72

"The name's Orley Hopper," said the skinny man, extending his hand. "I don't believe we've met before."

Matt could tell from the faint odor which hung around Hopper that he was a cowboy. There's not much else he could have been in that part of Colorado, anyway; this was cattle country, and almost every man in the bar was connected in some way with the ranching business. Most were cowpokes, Matt guessed.

"Pleased to meet you, Mr. Hopper. You can call me Matt—Matt Stanton." He shook the man's hand, noticing the remarkable strength of his grip.

"You can drop the 'mister.' Everybody just calls me Hopper most the time. What brings you to these parts, if you don't mind me askin'? You got folks around here?"

Another man probably would have put Matt on the defensive with a question like that, but there was something trustworthy about the skinny cowpoke that caused Matt to feel no discomfort in answering him, even though there was certainly no way to tell him the whole truth.

"No—I got no family. My pa died earlier this year. I guess that's why I'm roaming—there's really nothin' back where I come from for me to stay for. I thought maybe I could round up some work around here."

"Where you from, Matt?"

"Kentucky." Matt thought it might be best to not be too specific about his recent whereabouts. Trustworthy as Hopper seemed, there was no reason to say too much.

"Kentucky, you say? What's where my folks are from—well, I should say that's where they were before they headed through Cumberland Gap into

Tennessee. Most folks was goin' the other way, but mine decided to buck the trend and head south. We've been goin' backwards ever since, it seems." The lanky cowpoke leaned back his head and laughed at his own joke. It didn't strike Matt as all that funny, but the laughter was infectious and he joined in. It felt good to laugh; he hadn't done it in months, it seemed.

Matt accepted the other's invitation to a beer, then asked, "Which outfit you with, Hopper?"

"I work for the Jernigan ranch just northwest of here. Foreman." He took a long swallow of his beer, the foam clinging to his upper lip after he finished.

Foreman! Matt's heard raced at the word. Maybe this man could be more than just a drinking partner. Maybe he could get Matt some work.

"The Jernigan ranch—seems I've heard of it. Can't recall just where, though. That wouldn't be the one run by Ezra Jernigan, would it? From what I hear, he's one of the richest men west of the Mississippi."

"That's the one. His spread is one of the biggest in this area. You can stand on the south end and look north, and all the horizon you see is still a part of it. Lot of folks involved in the operation."

Hopper took another swallow of his beer, draining the glass. He caught the bartender's eye and waved the empty mug in the air for a refill. Matt sipped his more slowly, pondering the situation he was in and trying to think of some way to ask for work without trying to sound like he was taking advantage of Hopper's friendliness. He didn't want to sound pushy, or take advantage of a new-found friend, but his still partially empty

74

stomach and the ever-dwindling change in his pocket served as a constant reminder of how sorely he needed a job.

But as the conversation progressed, it seemed that the words would never come. The two men talked of a myriad of topics, and Matt tried to take advantage of any promising drift in the conversation, but he made no progress. It seemed the right opportunity just wouldn't come.

The saloon began to empty out around one in the morning. It was a far later-staying crowd than Matt would have expected, which rather surprised him until he remembered that this was a Saturday night. Most of the cowboys would have far less to do than their normal routine the next day. They might have only a scanty dose of religion in those parts, but they rarely failed to observe the Sabbath.

As the clock on the saloon wall chimed one-thirty, Orley Hopper began gathering up his jacket to leave. Matt was furious at himself for failing to ask about work, but now it seemed too late. Maybe tomorrow he could ride out to the ranch itself, but after missing such an opportunity as this that would seem a rather futile gesture. He tried not to let his anger at himself show as he bid goodnight to the skinny cowboy who had been his only friend since he parted ways with Will Monroe.

Hopper was halfway out the door when he turned to Matt and said, "By the way, if you'll stop by the Jernigan place about one tomorrow, I'll see what I can do about findin' you some work."

He was out of the door before Matt could choke out his thanks. He stood in flabbergasted shock for a few moments, then quietly smiled to himself. It seemed like the first good luck he had received in many days.

He would probably sleep in some deserted wood-shed tonight, but it didn't matter. With the prospect of work and a full stomach before him, the hard earth would be as comfortable as a feather mattress. He hummed a tune as he picked up his hat and headed out into the night.

9

Matt arose early the next morning, his excitement making sleep next to impossible. He was anxious to head for the Jernigan ranch, and the necessity of waiting until afternoon as Hopper had directed was a tantalizing torment. He fidgeted aimlessly for awhile, then decided he could best use the morning to make himself more presentable. His hair and beard were dirty and untrimmed, and he was in dire need of a bath.

He transformed the watering trough of the livery where he had slept into a makeshift bathtub before anyone came around. The water was cold and somewhat polluted, but after splashing around in the trough he felt much cleaner nonetheless. He washed out his clothes and hung them to dry in the morning sun before sitting down to trim his hair and beard with his knife.

After nearly an hour of wincing and bleeding he was not so much better-groomed as determined to sharpen the dull blade at his first opportunity. But his efforts managed to make him look somewhat more like a civilized human than a savage, and as for what he lacked in grooming—well, he told himself, cowboys aren't hired for looks.

When all his preparations were finished, he noticed with irritation that the sun was still low on the eastern horizon. Would the day never pass? He found loitering around the livery only made the minutes stretch longer, so long before noon he set out for the Jernigan ranch. At least he could wait out his time close to the place where he hoped to find work.

His nervousness decreased somewhat as he rode, and he sat straight in the saddle. The ranch was about an hour's ride from the town, and the moment he laid eyes on the ranch house his mouth opened and his eyes gaped in awe.

It looked as if one of the mansions of paradise had descended from above to set itself firmly down in the midst of the Colorado countryside. The structure was an imposing sight, three stories high and constructed of smoothly carved stone and timber. It looked completely incongruous there on the grasslands, but everything about it spoke of wealth and prestige, and Matt understood why the name of Ezra Jernigan was so well-known across the west.

Matt paused in a wooded area some distance from the house. The sun's position told him it was about noon, so he settled himself down for a rest until it was time for him to meet Hopper. As he waited he studied the area before him.

Around the main house, whose porch extended its entire width, were several smaller structures. Predominant among them was a long and low timbered structure, obviously the bunkhouse. There was little action or movement around any of the buildings, which Matt attributed to the fact that it was Sunday. Occasionally, though, an individual cowpoke or two would move in or out of one of the structures or toward the large circular corral nearby where several fine-looking horses were meandering restlessly about. Several barns stood close by, and beyond them stretched vast green pastureland that rose into rounded hills backed by green and brown timber stands.

There was no one around the ranch house itself for quite some time, but at length a young girl came around the far corner of the building and sat down on the shaded porch. Matt had to look close to tell it was a girl. She was dressed in a blue shirt and trousers, and her long brown hair was tied up behind her head. Watching from a distance as he was, Matt could not tell how old she was, but he guessed around the early or middle teens. His mind lazily pondered over who the girl might be. Jernigan's daughter? It seemed likely.

A little before one Matt mounted again and rode out from the sheltering trees toward the bunkhouse. The next few minutes would decide whether he worked or not. In spite of Hopper's encouraging statement of the previous night, Matt was sure that he would have to convince the boss himself—Ezra Jernigan—before his hiring would be official. His throat was dry and he had trouble keeping his hands from trembling as he grasped the reins and moved toward the bunkhouse.

He was pleased to see Hopper step from the blackness of the open bunkhouse as he drew near. At first the thin foreman didn't notice Matt, but when he halloowed a greeting the bronzed face looked up and twisted into a grin.

"Well, hello there, Matt. I was wonderin' if you would show up, but I see you're right on time."

Matt dismounted and tethered his horse to the corral fence. "Hello there, Hopper. I didn't get a chance to thank you for your offer last night. I guess you might say it took me by surprise." Matt shook the cowboy's hand. "To be right honest about it, I was thinkin' of askin' for work last night, but somehow I didn't get around to doin' it. I guess it didn't seem the right place."

"I could tell. You looked like a feller that could use a job, and them broad shoulders of yours should come in handy around here." Hopper paused. "Course you realize that I can't hire you without you checkin' with Ezra. He has the final say over all hirin', and since he's the one that does the payin' that only seems fair."

Matt nodded. "I expected that, and I'm ready to talk to him anytime he can see me." He tried not to look over-eager. "Did you mention I was comin'?"

"I told him there would be a young feller by askin' about work." He paused, then grinned in response to Matt's hopeful gaze. "Don't worry—I recommended you, told him I thought you would make a good hand. Mind you, though, that don't mean you're gonna get hired for sure. It ain't what I think of you that matters—it's what he thinks."

Hopper patted the young man on the shoulder. "We're just wastin' our time standin' out here and jawin' about it. Let's go have a talk with Ezra."

Matt grew more and more nervous as he approached the house, but he swallowed several times and determined to make the best of his opportunity. But when Hopper led the way into the spacious and elegant front room, it was all Matt could do to keep from shaking visibly.

His eyes scanned the fancy interior. The room was a conglomerate of mahogany, velvet, and deep, rich colors. Everywhere he looked Matt saw indications of great wealth. He fidgeted nervously, feeling utterly out of place amid such elegance. He couldn't imagine how someone could actually live in a place like this; it would be like dwelling in a house of cards, fearful that the slightest touch would destroy everything. Matt tried to avoid coming close to anything that looked expensive and breakable; the last thing he needed now was to shatter something priceless and irreplaceable. That wouldn't be likely to please Ezra Jernigan.

Hopper reached up and pulled a thin string that dangled beside the door. The faint tingling of the tiny bell on the end carried through the house. Matt waited expectantly for whoever it might summon. He glanced up toward the second floor landing across the room as he shifted nervously, and found his gaze returned by the same girl who he had seen earlier.

He had been right. She was in her mid-teens, but his earlier view from across the huge yard had done nothing to let him know how pretty she was. He gaped for a moment at her beauty, forgetting himself, then reddened slightly with embarrassment when the young girl turned and entered a second-floor room. He felt he must have looked rather ridiculous, standing there with his mouth open and his eyes staring, but he blamed it on the tension of the moment and looked back across the large room again.

He didn't dwell on the girl. Women had never played an important role in his life, with the exception of his mother, and right now he was far more interested in getting a regular job than thinking about some pretty child. After all, that's what she was—whoever she was. In a few brief moments she was forgotten.

When Ezra Jernigan walked into the room Matt knew immediately it was him. He was a tall, broad-shouldered man, graying slightly around the temples, yet somehow younger than Matt had expected. And his clothing was just as much in conflict with the room's elegant decor as Matt's and Hopper's. He was wearing old and dirty trousers, and his blue shirt was faded.

He had the look, nonetheless, of a distinguished man—one who was calm and capable of making big and important decisions in a short time with a minimum of worry. There was an air of authority about the man, an air that made him seem one who demanded respect yet remained unobtrusive and unassuming. Matt was humbled in his presence, but not extremely uncomfortable. He was determined not to botch his meeting with Jernigan, and the word "sir" hung at the tip of his tongue, ready to come out immediately and often.

Matt waited for Hopper to introduce him before he extended his hand at the moment the older gentleman did the same. "Ezra, this is Matt Stanton, the man I mentioned to you earlier. Matt, this is Mr. Ezra Jernigan."

Matt made sure his grip was firm when he shook hands with the smiling Jernigan. He wanted the man to be aware of his strength.

"Pleased to meet you, Matt."

"Mr. Jernigan—sir."

Hopper gestured toward Matt. "Matt here is lookin' for work. I think he'd make a good hand. We got a place we could use him?"

The tension was unbearable as Jernigan looked over the nervous young man for a long moment, sizing him up. He smilzed slightly, then looked over again at Hopper.

"If you think he can handle the work, we'll take him. We can always use a good hand."

It was as simple as that. Matt scarcely had time to thank the rancher before he turned and walked away, leaving Matt standing there incredulously. Not a question, not a moment of debate, and he had a job! It astounded him that it had all been so easy.

Hopper was grinning at the astonished young man, and he chuckled lightly. "Surprised? You'll get used to that once you get to know Ezra. He's never been one to take a long time to decide nothin'. He just moves and goes on from there. So far it's been a pretty good system for him." Hopper's eyes moved briefly around, sweeping significantly over the elegance surrounding the pair.

Matt looked for a moment at Hooper, then expressed his thanks to the foreman. He was so grateful that he could have hugged the skinny man's neck. It was as if Hopper had been an angel sent from above to bless Matt just when he needed it most.

"I'm awful obliged to you, Hopper. I'll try to do you a good job."

Hopper's calloused hand slapped him on the shoulder. "Don't mention it." He turned and exited through the front door, and Matt followed.

It was only as he walked toward the bunkhouse that the full impact began to sink in. He was hired—not by any two-bit outfit, either, but by one of the richest, biggest cattle empires west of the

Mississippi and east of the Rockies. The Jernigan ranch! Matt repeated the words over and over to himself, savoring the way they rolled over his tongue.

Hopper was whistling under his breath as he led Matt toward the bunkhouse. "Well, I guess you might as well get that saddle off your horse. It looks like you'll be stayin' awhile. I'll show you to your new home." His hand gestured toward the boarded building beside the corral.

As Matt carried the saddle toward the barn, Hopper asked him, "Just how much experience you got punchin' cattle, Matt?" Matt had expected the rather embarrassing question much sooner than this.

He wasn't sure how best to answer. "Well, to be right honest with you, Hopper," he stammered, "most of my experience has been with farmin' up 'til now. But I'm strong and a fast learner, and I promise you won't regret hirin' me." He paused, then asked the question that had been burning away at the back of his mind since the night before: "Why did you recommend me to Mr. Jernigan, not knowin' nothin' about me at all?"

Hopper smiled strangely and looked thoughtful. "Well, Matt, I always like to think I can tell the character of a man by lookin' at him, and if I got my guess right, you're a pretty good feller." He looked Matt over. "And to tell you the truth, there was a time I was in just your place. I got my first job from a young rancher I met in the same saloon we was in last night. It was years ago and he was just about as poor as I was. His name was Ezra Jernigan."

Matt said nothing, but from that moment on he

felt the pull of what promised to be a real friendship with Hopper. He entered the barn, tossed his saddle across a stall partition, then walked back out into the sunlight beside the lanky foreman.

"Let's head for the bunkhouse. There's an empty bunk beside the far wall. It'll be yours."

When he first entered the bunkhouse, Matt could see nothing for the darkness of the interior. The roughly hewn boards which made up the walls seemed to absorb every trace of light which filtered through the few small windows. There were coal-oil lamps here and there about the long room, but they were unlit. The walls were lined with simply designed bunks which gradually came into focus as his eyes adjusted to the dim light.

The place was filthy, dusty and dry. Discarded clothing was all over the floor, as well as draping many of the unmade bunks, whose linens consisted of a dirty pillow and one or two rough blankets. Most of the beds appeared to be straw ticks. The room was empty, the inhabitants either out on various parts of the ranch or in town enjoying a free afternoon.

But the most noticeable feature of the bunkhouse was its rather pungent and unique smell—a mixture of sweat, tobacco, coffee, dust, cow—and cowboy. Matt couldn't help turning up his nose at the biting odor, and he wondered how he could ever live in a place like this. He had never seen such a trash-heap before. He tried to comfort himself by thinking that even this was better than sleeping in woodsheds or beneath the stars with empty pockets. Maybe he would get used to the odor.

Hopper apparently had, for he didn't even seem

to notice the smell as he pointed Matt toward an empty bunk on the far end of the bunkhouse. Matt threw his saddlebags and bedroll down on the bunk, noticing with some pleasure that it had apparently been unused before and so was not as dirty and unappealing as the others.

"Well, this will be your home as long as you're with us," Hopper said. "And I hope you can sleep with snorin' goin' on, 'cause at night this place rumbles like the Abilene cattle trains."

"Can't be worse than the places I've been stayin' lately," Matt commented. "This is the closest thing to luxury I've had in a long time." He tried to make the words sound convincing as his nose continued to rebel at the foul odor.

He sat down on the bunk, testing it. "How long you been with Mr. Jernigan, Hopper?"

The cowboy looked reflective. "Sixteen years, though it sure don't seem that long. I was with him when he started out, and I've been with him through everything else—when he married, when he had his daughter. . ."

"Was that the girl that was upstairs in the house?"

"That's her—and she's a feisty little devil, let me tell you. More energy than a half-grown kitten! I've been with her ever since she was born, guess I feel like she's halfway mine. I think she's just as much jack as she is jenny. I never saw such a tomboy!"

"They got any other children?"

"No—would have had a son, but he died at birth about ten years ago. I don't expect they'll have any others."

Hopper sat down on the bunk next to Matt's, his

eyes thoughtful. Matt guessed he was living over his old times in his head, the days when he and Ezra Jernigan carved out a successful cattle empire here in the wild Colorado countryside. He broke from his reverie quickly, and looked at Matt.

"Well, boy, I'm ready for my dinner. I'm as hungry as a starved bear. Let's go see if we can round us up some chow."

Matt was agreeable to the proposition, and the two headed back out into the midday sunshine.

10

Spring, 1879. More than four million cattle were spread across the west, grazing on the rich prairie grasses. Ranches ranged from huge empires to much smaller enterprises, some consisting of only a few acres of grassland bordering a river. The cattle business was thriving, and the trains at Denver, Ellsworth, Dodge City, and the other cattle towns were shipping out load after load of longhorns to the east, where they would be sold at ten times the price they would bring in the west.

One of the largest of the Colorado cattle empires was the Jernigan ranch, which had vastly increased its already substantial holdings over the past few years. The wealth amassed by the ranch was almost uncountable, and Ezra Jernigan controlled an area of grazing land that could swallow up certain eastern states in its vastness. He did not own it all personally—some was gained through his cowboys taking out homestead claims along the choice riverfront lands. Nevertheless he ran it, and the thousands of cattle roaming his lands annually added tremendous sums to his income, and his men drove huge herds of the bawling animals to the railroad centers in Denver and Pueblo each year.

Many men came and went at the ranch, working sometimes only one or two drives before moving elsewhere. Others stayed on as regular workers. Orley Hopper was one, and Matt was another. It was six years now since he had hired on at the ranch. His lowly rank as a cowboy had quickly changed; by 1876 he was assistant foreman and integral not only in the manual labor involved in running a ranch but in the business dealings as well. He was a trusted ally to his two superiors, and they trusted his judgement almost as much as their own. When he had come to the job he had been a tenderfoot, as green as they come, but he had learned his job well, and it had paid off.

For the first few months after he hired on he had felt that the whole world consisted of sore legs, aching muscles, a bruised backside, dust-irritated eyes, and the never-ending smell of hot, dirty cattle. Matt had found himself in an endless cycle of days filled with nothing but hard work and nights plagued with dreams of bawling, rolling masses of longhorns. Never before had he imagined that the life of a cowpoke would consist of such dreary toil, such eternal labor. There had been moments when his time as a starving drifter almost seemed a blissful existence compared to this.

But in his heart he knew how ridiculous such thoughts were, and he often reminded himself of how fortunate he really was, in spite of the dreary and painful labor. From the outset he determined to become the best cowboy employed by Jernigan, and it was a determination he never forgot. His efforts did not go unnoticed by Orley Hopper and Ezra Jernigan. It was because of his hard work and dedication that he attained the status at the ranch which he now held.

Somewhere in the six years that had passed the last traces of impetuous youth had almost totally vanished from Matt, draining out slowly, imperceptibly, like the summer green of a hickory leaf gradually changing to autumn gold. The earlier restlessness which had stirred so wildly within him had hidden itself in the recesses of his mind, and the clear rationality that comes with maturity had replaced it by degrees. Without being conscious of the change, Matt had grown from a hot-tempered young firebrand into a calm and mature adult who was not swayed easily by raw emotion but who instead thought things through before he acted. It was a trait he had picked up from Orley Hopper, though neither he nor the lanky cowbody ever realized it.

Eventually Matt had found the hard-working life of a cowboy becoming more comfortable, and now he did not dread the mornings like he did at first. He knew that it was not the work that had changed so much, but himself instead. His muscles were toughened and hardened now, as was his resolve to do his best at whatever job he had to tackle. Ezra Jernigan was well pleased with the man Matt Stanton had become.

But there was another member of the Jernigan household who was even more delighted with the young cowboy. When Matt had come to the ranch, Melissa Jernigan had paid no more heed to Matt than he had to her. They had gone about their lives almost oblivious to each other, Matt concerned with learning his new profession and Melissa with resisting her mother's attempts to turn her from a tomboy to a lady.

But during that six years since Matt had first come, she had grown into a beautiful young woman. Her brown hair was long and shining and her skin was fair and unblemished. Her eyes were as deeply brown as her hair and sparkled in a beautifully-featured face, and her figure had changed from the skinny, boyish form of a youngster to the delicate and attractive shape of a lovely young lady.

Her beauty did not escape Matt's notice, and by the time she was twenty, he was deeply and helplessly in love. Happily, his love was not unrequited, for Melissa grew to cherish the shy cowboy whose clumsy attempts at courtship seemed so sincere and touching to her. Ezra and Sally Jernigan were pleased with the romance between their daughter and Matt, and often they discussed the matter in hushed, happy voices upon their bed at night.

Matt took a lot of kidding about his love affair, but in spite of the embarrassment it sometimes caused him, he rarely responded in anger. He felt that Melissa Jernigan was worth the harassment, and he was continually conscious of how fortunate he was to court her. There was no doubt in his mind—it was love he felt for the rancher's daughter.

Many times lately Matt had to stop and ponder the strange workings of fate. It was a strangely convoluted road he had traveled. He began with a happy though impoverished family in the Kentucky mountains, then moved on to Kansas where he lost his mother and his father, then came his life as a free and unwanted man. Then when things were at their worst he found a job, and now the addition of Melissa to his life was making things look bright again.

Never in his life had Matt loved a woman, indeed, he had hardly known any woman at all, living as he had the life of a prairie youth. He had never been one to dwell on romance; he had gone through his youth and young manhood assuming that he would live single all his life.

Now, in the prime of life, love had unexpectedly struck him. He knew that he could never be free of his devotion to the beautiful Colorado girl, but if love like that was bondage, it was a bondage he craved. He hoped to marry her someday, and he saved every extra penny toward that goal.

He felt sure Melissa knew of his intentions, and he had little doubt that she would enter willingly into a marriage to him. It was obvious that her affection toward him was every bit as strong as the love he felt for her.

But as of yet he had been unable to ask her that most important question. Not that he hadn't tried—it just seemed that the words stuck in his throat every time he tried to force them out. The courage that had held fast during the perilous jail-break at Briar Creek and the close call with the posse in Jimmy's shed could not survive the gaze of a beautiful girl. It was somewhat ludicrous, even funny, Matt realized in his more objective moments, but somehow he couldn't laugh.

ii

It was well into spring. The winter chill was almost gone now, lingering only at night, and the hills had turned from a dull brown to a deep, luscious green. Across the plains the cattle were grazing on the new growth, growing fat after the lean winter days.

Ezra Jernigan was making plans, organizing his men, and doing all the preliminary work necessary before one of the most massive operations of his ranch commenced. The trains would be waiting at Denver one day to take on his herd which was now scattered over countless acres of grasslands, roaming free and wild over the open plains of the Jernigan ranch. There were new calves to be branded.

The roundup would be a major task, requiring all of the men Jernigan alrady had hired, and probably many more. So springtime heralded to the cowboys not only warmer, more pleasant days, but also the prospect of hard, dusty labor amid bawling cattle that had grown accustomed to the free life on the plains and felt absolutely no desire to be herded or branded.

It would not be an easy task, but it was the lifeblood of the Jernigan ranch and all those who depended on it. In past years Matt had dreaded each roundup and the autumn drive, but now he had grown to accept it as part of the regular routine of his life. The hard part now was not the labor, but enduring the long separation from Melissa that went along with it.

He knew he would miss her terribly during those long days and nights out on the plains, but he also realized that most of his hours would be so busy that he would have little time for self-pity. That would make it a little easier, but even then it would be difficult to be so far from her, temporary though the separation would be. But such was the life of a cowboy, and there was nothing to do but accept it.

Accept it—and take advantage of every free moment before the roundup began to be with her. Matt found himself rushing through his work now in order to have more time to see her. The other cowboys took note and redoubled their harassment of their lovestricken friend. Matt especially received ridicule for his habit of taking a bath every chance he got, no matter how inconvenient. Unlike his friends, he couldn't afford to be careless about his personal cleanliness.

"Look at 'im—cleanest drover in Colorado," they would laugh. "What's the matter, Matt? Can't you stand your own smell? You scrub any more and I swear you're gonna take off the hide!"

The abuse was as endless as it was good-natured. Matt took it into his usual stride, getting angry only once—the time Hopper threw a stinking heap of fresh horse manure on his head the moment he finished his bath. But the joking never got beyond the verbal stage, and Matt knew full well that he would be just as rough on one of his own friends should their roles be reversed.

So Matt and Melissa spent all the time they could together, though Matt's duties made their time scarce. But the scarcity only increased the preciousness of their shared moments, so they complained little.

But the night before the drive was to begin Melissa cried and would not be comforted. Matt tried to soothe her, but the effort was futile, for he shared the same feelings, though he hid them inside. Eventually he gave up trying to comfort the girl, and they sat without words together beneath the stars in the front yard of the Jernigan house.

It was then that Ezra Jernigan called Matt back to the house. Matt knew that whatever he had to say must be important, for he was not in the habit of disturbing the pair when they were together.

Jernigan got straight to the point. "Matt, Spencer has finally decided to sell out that riverfront grazin' land I've been tryin' to get so long. That'll be a choice addition to our holdin's, and I can't afford to pass up the chance to buy him out. The trouble is, he can't be here 'til Monday, which bums up my plan to go along with the rest of the men tomorrow."

Matt waited wordlessly for Jernigan's point.

"I'll need you and Hopper to stay behind with me," he said. "After I close the deal I want us to ride out there and look over the land. I'm thinkin' it might be a good spot to build some sort of dwellin', you know, to place a man out there regular, maybe several men. This ranch is gettin' so big that it's hard to use this place here as a main base for all of it. We need to start spreadin' out our center of operations a little more. But I don't want to make a final decision without you and Hopper bein' in on it. So it looks like it'll be a few more days before the three of us can head out after the others. We'll let Hardy head it up 'til we get there—he's capable enough, I think."

Matt agreed, and the decision was made. And when he returned to the yard where Melissa still sat and shared the news with her, her tears came all the faster, though now they were a product of joy rather than grief.

Melissa kissed Matt hard and long when the tears finally stopped. She knew that he was just as happy about the delay as she was. During that time they would have opportunities to be together—much more than they normally would, for with the bulk of the men out on the trail there would be little that could be done around the ranch, and Matt would be relieved of many of his regular obligations, at least until Monday when the man named Spencer arrived to sell his land. It was Friday now, so that gave the couple two extra days to be together.

Sunday would be the best of those days, for it was the one time during the week when virtually no work was done on the ranch. The pious and strong-willed Sally Jernigan made sure of that—as long as she was the wife of Ezra Jernigan there would be no violating the Lord's Day on this particular ranch—and although Ezra Jernigan griped and fumed about his wife's mandate, he never challenged it. When it came to Sundays, Sally Jernigan reigned supreme, a veritable divine-right monarch. So after the morning service in nearby Wilson's Fork let out, Matt and Melissa would have an afternoon to call their own—and they intended to make the best of it. The fact that the extra time was unexpected made it all the more precious.

Th next morning the roundup began. A huge party of cowpokes loped out of the corral and on across the plains, heading for the pre-determined location at which they would divide into smaller groups to scour the plains for longhorns which they would drive back to the same spot where they had broken up. Then would come the branding.

Only Hopper, Matt, and Jernigan remained behind with the women, the maid, the cook, and the gardener. The ranch seemed incredibly empty, and that night both Hopper and Matt had trouble sleeping in the cavernous bunkhouse without the usual serenade of loud and grating snores to which they had become accustomed.

Join the Western Book Club
and GET 4 FREE* BOOKS NOW!
A $19.96 VALUE!

Yes! I want to subscribe to the Western Book Club.

Please send me my **4 FREE* BOOKS**. I have enclosed $2.00 for shipping/handling. Each month I'll receive the four newest Leisure Western selections to preview for 10 days. If I decide to keep them, I will pay the Special Members Only discounted price of just $3.36 each, a total of $13.44, plus $2.00 shipping/handling ($19.50 US in Canada). This is a **SAVINGS OF AT LEAST $6.00** off the bookstore price. There is no minimum number of books I must buy, and I may cancel the program at any time. In any case, the **4 FREE* BOOKS** are mine to keep.

*In Canada, add $5.00 shipping/handling per order
for the first shipment. For all future shipments to
Canada, the cost of membership is $16.25 US,
which includes shipping and handling.
(All payments must be made in US dollars.)

NAME: _____

ADDRESS: _____

CITY: _____ STATE: _____

COUNTRY: _____ ZIP: _____

TELEPHONE: _____

E-MAIL: _____

SIGNATURE: _____

11

i

The eyes that watched the string of mounted cowboys moving steadily toward the hills and rolling plains beyond the main portion of the Jernigan ranch were hard eyes—cold and emotionless.

Hidden by the thick spring leaves of the brush in which they sat mounted, their horses quietly grazing on the tender grass between their hooves, were four men who watched the moving band of drovers without a word. But in the grim lines of their faces and the serious gaze of their eyes it was obvious that they were anything but unconcerned watchers of the panoramic scene before them. There was purpose in the way they gazed at the string of cowboys.

Two of the men were young, their faces hardly bearded despite the fact that they had not shaved for weeks now. There was almost a boyish look in their faces, though already the toughening life of the trail was putting wrinkles around the corners of their eyes and a deep, leather-like bronze in their skin. But their youth did not hide the cold aura about them, something which spoke of experience in vice beyond their years.

One was blonde, the other sandy-haired, though the dust of the Colorado plains was so thick in their unwashed hair that the tints were almost indistinguishable. The same dust coated the clothes and skin of the other two men, one apparently in his forties, the other seeming much older, his hair and beard snowy white and long and his shoulders stooped as if with a great burden. His bearing was weary, but there was something powerful in the stoop of his broad shoulders and a strength in his form which would have identified him immediately to any observer as the leader of the group.

They sat for a long time, watching the cowboys in the valley move farther and farther away until the last straggler was almost out of sight. Then the white-haired leader tossed his head slightly, and the four men turned their horses and moved silently away from the edge of the hill.

They began to ride at a steady pace in the opposite direction of the cowboys, heading toward the Jernigan ranch.

ii

Matt could not remember a more beautiful spring day. The sky was clear and the sun was warm and shining brilliantly, warming the spring breeze that blew gently against his face. And seated in the horse-drawn buggy with her arm entwined with his was Melissa, a smile on her face and her shining brown hair blowing slightly behind her as the buggy moved down the road at a rapid clip.

It was Sunday afternoon, and though Jernigan and Hopper had finally convinced the piously reluctant Sally Jernigan to allow them to spend the afternoon on some necessary paperwork, Matt had been excused. Although he had said nothing of it, Jernigan had sensed his daughter's desire to be with her lover on their last opportunity for quite some time, and he had sent them off for an afternoon together with no obligations but to enjoy the other's presence.

Matt had rigged up the buggy as fast as possible and they had started straight for Walker's Creek, their favorite spot, a few miles from the Jernigan house. They were determined to not waste one moment of the precious time that was left them, time neither had expected only a few days before.

The couple were jovial, laughing and singing loudly and ridiculously as the horse trotted along. Matt felt giddy joy rippling through him. The present was so real, and Melissa so delightful, that bad times seemed only a hazy, distant dream. Life was good right now, unbelievably good.

It was only moments after they arrived at the little wooded nook through which the cool, bubbling spring waters flowed that Melissa kicked off her shoes and waded out into the rippling stream, laughing with the innocent delight of a child. Matt headed in after her, his heart as young and carefree as hers, laughing, calling to her, playfully splashing her fleeing form with water as she did the same to him. How could he help but love this beautiful young lady who took such delight in pleasures as simple as the feeling of cool spring waters flowing around her feet? His heart overflowed with love, and his hands reached out to her and drew her to him.

Their lips met as their arms entwined and their minds grew intoxicated with the kiss of the other. All else around them disappeared, the cool waters no longer noticed. The sole reality became the other, the one pressing so close in love.

Melissa felt that surely this was the moment—this was the time he would ask the question she so longed to hear. But he said nothing. It seemed he could not ask her. Could it be that he did not love her with the same fervor with which she loved him? She refused to believe it—she couldn't. She tried to force the doubt away as she fell into the oblivion toward which his kiss drew her. She told herself that when the time was right, he would ask her to become his bride. That hope was essential to her; without it she could not go on.

And yet—and yet—the doubt lingered. So long she had waited, so many times she had prayed for that one question that would fulfill her deepest desire. But he would never ask. Everything seemed so perfect, but he wouldn't ask.

She knew he was shy—her courtship had taught her that much. Affection was hard for him to show, yet that only made his halting expressions of love all the more beautiful to her. But in spite of that she couldn't grasp why he would not give out that final expression of love. She wanted so badly to become his wife; she dreamed of it often. Maybe one day it would really be—maybe.

Melissa forced herself to control her thoughts. She had no desire to ruin the afternoon with doubts and imaginings. Perhaps in her eagerness to marry Matt she was rushing things along too quickly. They were still young, there was no need for haste. This afternoon together was far too precious to waste with needless sadness.

So Melissa forced herself back to the real world and smiled at Matt with shining eyes. She pushed her doubts away by the sheer strength of her will. Her eyes betrayed her moments before she playfully stomped her foot in the water, sending spray in all directions and drenching both herself and Matt.

Matt laughed and tried to sweep her up in his arms, but the nimble girl evaded him and ran laughing downstream, lifting her skirts slightly to avoid wetting them. The effort was unsuccessful. Matt chased her, his feet raising huge splashes of water all around him.

As he caught her, they fell, his body landing atop hers in the cool, shallow water. For a moment he feared he had hurt her, but her joyous laugh relieved his worry. Their eyes came together and Matt gazed at her rosy-cheeked face. Even when she was drenched and breathless she was beautiful.

He kissed her, then again and again. Her kiss weakened him and made him tremble there in the rushing water. He would have remained there for long minutes, lost in her embrace had she not broken through his trance with words edged in laughter: "Don't you think we would be more comfortable out of the water?"

Matt gazed at her rather stupidly for a moment, then felt his face reddening with embarrassment.

"Sorry. I guess I wasn't thinkin' too straight."

As they walked to the bank, Matt slipped his arm around the slender waist of his lover. Both of them were soaked, but the sun was warm and the breeze only slightly chilling. Matt had to smile to himself as he realized how very at ease he felt with this beautiful girl. How he loved her!

The couple spent the afternoon walking together, talking quietly, each dreaming of the future. The day seemed far too short, and it was already beginning to grow dark when they started back to the house, grateful for the time they had spent together and sad that it could not continue.

Melissa found it hard to hold back tears as she rode in the buggy seat beside Matt toward the house. She was aware the he would leave the next day, and she was painfully conscious of the long time they would be separated. The ranch would seem so lonely and empty when he was gone.

Matt bade her goodnight on the front porch and Melissa walked slowly to her room. She felt very alone.

Her gaze swept the room for no particular reason, lingering on the oak wardrobe standing in the corner. She stared at it blankly, seeing but not noticing that the door was slightly ajar. She stood silently for awhile, her arms wrapped around herself to block out the cool night breeze. She became suddenly conscious of the draft blowing through the room. Where was it coming from? She turned rather absently toward the window.

It was open. It took a minute to sink in. She had left it shut that morning—someone must have opened it in her absence. The maid? Maybe, but nevertheless, she felt a strange and gripping apprehension as she moved toward the window.

She paused there for a moment, looking across the dark yard toward the woods beyond. The moonlight was dim, clouds obscuring its brilliance.

But something caught her eye in the darkness, over near the trees. Was that a man she saw, holding the bridle of a horse and staring toward the house? Or was it more than one? Who could they be, and why were they here on the ranch after all the men had left?

Alarm stirred inside her, and she breathed faster as she turned away from the window. She had to tell her father what she had seen. Those men shouldn't be there—the ranch was supposed to be empty but for the women, servants, and the three men who stayed behind.

She turned from the window and stared speechless with shock into the leering face of a dirty, middle-aged man in rough garb. A filthy and battered hat sat atop his head, and his beard was a scrubby coal pile. He said nothing but grabbed the young girl, pressing a powerful hand over her mouth to choke off her scream. Behind him the wide-open door of the wardrobe betrayed his former hiding place.

Never had Melissa experienced such total and sudden horror. This was unreal, impossible! Who was this sweaty, stinking man who held her? And what were his intentions? Her muscles tensed and her heart raced.

Her father was only a short distance away, in his room with her mother. But how could she tell him what was happening? The hand crushed over her mouth and throat made screaming impossible. She began stomping her foot on the hardwood floor, trying to make as much noise as possible.

The man cursed beneath his breath, then picked her up off the floor, slipping his arm behind her knees and sweeping her up. His other hand still pressed against her mouth, blocking any noise. He shoved his dirty, bearded face close to hers and whispered roughly, "Shut up—one more noise and you'll be dead. I'll choke you before you have time to think. And if you manage to get anyone else into this room, there's men outside that'll blow their heads right off, right through the window here. You got that, missy?"

Melissa looked with frightened eyes at the ugly face above her, then quickly nodded her head. The man grinned evilly, then began moving toward the window, the girl still in his arms. He sat her on the floor, then forced her head backward until the back of her neck rested on the sill of the window, her long hair trailing outside into the darkness. His hand covered her mouth until she felt the tip of something sharp against her exposed throat.

"One noise and I'll slit your pretty throat—understand?"

His hand moved away from her mouth then, and two other hands from outside came up on either side of her head. She felt something being stuffed into her mouth and a bandana was pulled tightly across it and tied roughly behind her head. All the while the man above her was grinning an evil and disturbing smile.

"Well, missy, you're all trussed up real good now, ain't you? Now get up, slow and quiet, and climb on out the window. Make any noise and the first thing I'll do is head down the hall and slice up your ma. That's a promise."

Melissa did as she was told. Strong hands grabbed her as soon as she was outside. She felt herself being picked up and thrown over a shoulder like a sack of feed. Then she was carried quickly across the yard in the direction of the woods.

An understanding of what was happening began to form in her terrified brain. She was being kidnapped, taken by this band of men. No doubt they had left some sort of ransom instructions in her room for her parents to find. Even the possibility of such a happening had never come to her mind, yet now it was a dreadful, awful reality. And all the while her father, Matt, and Hopper, the men who could save her, were only a short distance away, totally unaware of what was happening.

She was tossed onto the back of a horse, and a gruffly barked order to ride set it in motion. Into the night she moved, the wind whipping her hair and the whole incredible situation seeming like a horrible nightmare. Maybe, she thought, that's what it was. God, how she hoped so! But in her heart she knew it was no dream.

As the band of riders forced her horse onward, carrying her farther and farther from the house, she thought of Matt, her father, her mother. When would they discover her absence? It could be morning before anyone looked into her room, and by then she would be carried miles away. And who were these men that had taken her? So far she had seen only one face, and she didn't recognize it.

She strained her eyes in the darkness and looked at the single rider before her. The other three were behind, making sure her horse kept up its speed. She could see nothing but his back, and the only feature she could notice was his long white hair, whipping wildly behind him as he rode.

12

It took a full hour to quiet Sally Jernigan, who had gone almost immediately into hysterics when she learned what had happened. Jernigan tried to comfort his wife, assuring her that he would bring her back their daughter, but his words had little effect. Perhaps it was because of his own lack of assurance of their truth, and his own shock at the unbelievable event which had occurred.

Jernigan had never seriously faced the possibility that something like this might happen, and he cursed himself for his lack of forethought. He was a wealthy man, and there were greedy and desperate men in the world who would do almost anything to get a part of his money. But to harm his family—to actually steal away his daughter, leaving behind only a terse and chilling ransom letter—he had never conceived of such a thing happening. But yet it had, so silently and swiftly that neither he nor anyone else in the house had noticed. He had seen this kind of thing before; he felt a fool for not realizing it could just as easily happen to him as other men.

Matt's mind was a dark quandry of bitter anger.

He couldn't even form his thoughts into words; feelings ran through him like a rampaging torrent, shifting and fluctuating before he could verbalize them even to himself. The bitter irony of it all was the worst part—the shattering of his naive belief that he had left all the pain in his life behind at Briar Creek. But now the only girl he had ever loved was taken from him, just like everything else that had meant anything to him in the past. It seemed that life could be endlessly cruel.

He condemned himself for his selfish thoughts. Could he think only of himself? He knew the torment must be far greater for Melissa, taken by strangers who might do anything to her without hesitation, and who had no concern for her except the extent to which they could profit from her wealthy father. But anymore, her pains, pleasures, and desires were so entwined with Matt's that they were virtually indistinguishable. It was not only for himself but for Melissa that he hurt.

Hopper remained silent through most of the morning, but later on he said to his friend, in private, "Matt, you know we have to do something about this."

"Of course I do. Right now we're just wastin' our time standin' around here and talkin' about it. They can't be far gone—they've only had one night's jump on us. We ought to be able to catch up to 'em soon—to fight 'em and get Melissa back."

"Wait a minute, Matt. I was hopin' you wouldn't be thinkin' like that, but I guess it could be expected, as close as you are to the girl. Stop and think a minute—why would they wait 'til last night to take her? They've probably been around for days."

Matt paused, thinking, and what Hopper was driving at struck him suddenly. "The roundup—all the men are gone from the ranch, except the house workers—and they think that we're gone with 'em! They couldn't have known that we stayed behind." Matt paused again. "That means that they don't think there's anybody here to follow 'em."

Hopper nodded. "That's right. Which means we've got the element of surprise on our side. The thing for us right now is to not let them know that there's anybody on this ranch right now that could be a threat to them. They'll be more careless that way. The way I've got it figured they think somebody here will have to go out after all the men that took out on the roundup, and by now they're two days away. Then it would be two more days for 'em to get back here before anyone could follow those scoundrels."

Matt admired Hopper's clear thinking as the cowboy continued. "The only thing that surprises me is that they didn't wait a little longer before they took the girl. My guess is that they just got a little anxious, maybe a little jumpy. Still, it's a sensible plan they have, but we can use the fact that they don't know we're here to our advantage."

"You don't think we should just sit here, do you Hopper? You sounded like you didn't like the idea of goin' after 'em."

" 'Course we should go after 'em. But we don't need to take out of here like a stampede and tip our hand to 'em. The thing for us to do is follow a long ways off, maybe even until they reach where they're goin'. They'll figure that whoever comes to deliver that ransom will be at least a week behind.

Besides the time it'll take, according' to their thinkin', for anybody to get back here from the roundup, they're probably countin' on some slack time for Ezra to round up the ransom money. I ain't seen the letter, but the maid told me they're demandin' fifty thousand in cash. Even for someone like Ezra, that much money is hard to round up all at once."

Matt scratched his chin. "But don't they figure the whole lot of Mr. Jernigan's men will take out after 'em? There's got to be more of us than them, if you count all the extra hands hired on for the roundup. Seems like they couldn't expect nothin' but an army of drovers ridin' in on 'em later and takin' Melissa by force. Why would they take such a risk?"

"Because they know Ezra ain't gonna do nothin' to place his daughter in danger," Hopper answered. "He would never sent in a big bunch of armed men to try and take her, 'cause them kidnappers would likely just kill her first thing. Nope, they ain't got to worry about no army of drovers. Ezra will never do nothin' like that."

Ezra Jernigan walked into the room. His face was ashen and his eyes were vacant and hollow. Neither Matt nor Hopper spoke, not knowing what to say to a man whose daughter had just been stolen away. Jernigan sat down heavily in a chair and looked up into the faces of the two men before him. Despair hung around him like a dismal fog.

"Well, men, what do you suggest we do?"

Matt fidgeted slightly, not knowing how to answer. Hopper spoke out after a moment.

"I think we ought to go after 'em, Ezra."

The rancher nodded his head wearily. "I agree.

There's no time to waste goin' out after the men on the roundup. And there's no law to speak of in Wilson's Fork to give us a hand. We'll go alone. I guess you two have already figured out that they don't realize we're here now.'' Hopper and Matt nodded.

"You two were discussing a plan when I walked in. Would you fill me in on it?''

Hopper repeated what he had said to Matt, and Jernigan nodded as he listened. Then he looked closely at the two men, obviously about to say something worth hearing.

"I don't think we should take any ransom money.''

Matt's jaw dropped when he heard that, and before he could restrain himself he burst out, "No ransom money! Why, they'll kill Melissa for sure, then!'' Matt was shocked. Had the rancher lost his mind?

Jernigan shook his head firmly. "No, Matt, they won't kill her any quicker than they would anyway,'' he said. "This ransom wouldn't stop 'em from killin' her, not for a minute. I've seen two situations similar to this in my life, and in both cases the person was killed in spite of the ransom. No sir. I plan to take my daughter back alive. I'll not pay to see her killed.''

He stood, his face looking stronger as he spoke with determination. "It would take me at least three days to round up fifty thousand dollars in cash, then we would take the risk of having it robbed while we carried it to 'em. Then likely they would kill Melissa and whoever took 'em the money, too. We've got surprise on our side, and they only have a little jump on us. The thing for us to do is follow 'em like Hopper suggested and surprise 'em later. By the way, since neither of you have read the ransom letter, do you know where we're supposed to deliver the money? Matt and Hopper shook their heads.

Jernigan paused, looking deeply at the two before answering. "Beggar's Gulch."

Matt's mouth fell open and Hopper let out a slow, awed whistle. Beggar's Gulch was the most notorious hideout for human scum in the state of Colorado. It was the site of a former monastery, known to the Spanish settlers near it as The Place of the Virgin. It had been set up by and order of Texas-based priests who served years before as missionaries to the Indians. But it had fallen into other hands long ago, and there was hardly an outlaw who at sometime or another had not taken refuge within the high walls of the monastery in the box canyon called Beggar's Gulch. No one had gone near the place in years, with the exception of a few brave though foolhardy lawmen who had never returned. The story had come back lately that the place was deserted, no outlaws hiding there.

But Melissa was being taken to the monastery, so apparently that rumor was no longer true. Someone must have reoccupied the old walled monastery, and now Matt, Hopper, and Jernigan were to be forced to ride right into it. It was a place Matt had never expected to see, but now it seemed he might. Beggar's Gulch. The very name sent a chill down his spine.

"My Lord!" exclaimed Hopper. "The idea of anyone taking Melissa there. . ." His voice trailed off into incredulity, and his eyes stared blankly as he pondered the situation.

"It's gonna be hard to get her out if they get her inside that wall," Jernigan said. "But I don't think it'll be safe to try and take her on the trail. Once they get to the monastery they'll figure they're safe and free from pursuit for several days, and maybe they'll let down their guard a little. But as long as they're on the trail, they're gonna be careful. Nope—I don't think it'll do to make our move 'til they get to Beggar's Gulch. We've got to preserve that element of surprise. If we get an especially good chance on the trail, we'll take it. But if they spot us, then Melissa would be—" He didn't finish the sentence, but everyone knew what he would have said.

Hopper looked around at the other two. "The quicker we get goin' the better chance we'll have. If it's all right with you, Ezra, I'll go and saddle up the horses. Beggar's Gulch is a good five days ride, if not more. We're gonna be delayed enough as it is, havin' to hang back so they don't spot us. Matt, you go and stock up some travelin' food for us."

They left Jernigan alone in the room as they headed out to do their tasks. The whole thing seemed unreal to Matt; it was as if at any moment he would slip out of this waking dream into the bright world he had known only the day before, with Melissa beside him and everything fine. But the nightmare continued, unending.

And almost imperceptible in the darkest shadows of his mind there stirred feelings that had lay hidden for six years now—feelings of hatred, anger, and the overwhelming desire for vengeance. Scenes from his past played through his mind— visions of the flaming farm at Briar Creek, his father's dead body, the evil grin of Marcus Leach and the kick of the pistol in his hand when he had killed him. He thought of Monroe, of Jimmy—and then of Melissa. He knew the fire inside him would never be cooled until he had her back again, and until those that had taken her had paid in full for their crime.

The trio set off before noon, heading along the trail left by the kidnappers. They felt encouraged when they only made out the trail of five horses. Maybe there were less of them than they would have guessed.

The day dragged on slowly, the men hardly speaking to one another. The things that had occupied their minds for days now—the cattle roundup, the purchase of the Spencer land—all of these things seemed distant now, and meaningless. One thing mattered: the life of the beautiful and gentle girl who had been stolen.

And so as Matt's eyes scanned the trail before him, it seemed he could see only one thing, and it wouldn't go out of his mind—the deep brown eyes of Melissa Jernigan, perhaps gone from him forever.

13

Melissa could cry no longer. It was as if she had drained herself empty; nothing more could come. A kind of bitter resignation had settled on her, a hellish acceptance of the misery in which she existed. It had been only three days since she had been taken, yet it seemed as though she could not remember her ˙life before. Her whole existence seemed to have been lived out in the past three pain-filled days, days that had stretched on like months.

Prior to that her memory drew up only a haze panorama of a previous life, a life of happiness and peace with her family. But it was vague, like a scene viewed through ˙a fog, and there was no connection between that life to the one she now lived. Or was it life at all that she now endured? Perhaps this was death. It might as well have been, she felt, for surely there was nothing but pain left for her now.

Even in the brilliant noonday sunshine Melissa felt as if she were enveloped in blackness, dark as a starless night. Only one light shone to her in that darkness—the face of Matt Stanton. The memory of that face was all she had to sustain her now, to keep her from losing her straining sanity. Only the image of his clear blue eyes kept her from yielding up what little hope she had left.

Yet there were times when even that image was blocked out, replaced by other eyes—eyes that burned with a light stranger than any she had ever seen. They belonged to the white-haired leader of the band that had taken her, and often she felt herself compelled to look deeply into them, transfixed as if by a hypnotic light that blazed in their depths.

What was it about the man that so unnerved her? There was something wrong in his gaze, something strange and abnormal. When he spoke, and that was rare, his words were troubled and halting, as if somehow she caused in him the same unsettledness that he aroused in her.

What plagued her so was that she knew full well she had never seen this man before, yet the gaze which he so often fixed on her looked like nothing else than a straining attempt to recognize her. It seemed as if he were trying to call up into his mind the identity of this girl riding with him. And once he whispered a name under his breath, a name she couldn't make out but which she knew was not her own. Yet Melissa knew that he was aware of who she was—he had to be. He was the man who led the group that had taken her. He had to know who she was.

She knew they were asking fifty thousand dollars for her life. She had heard it from one of the younger men in the group, the blonde one they called Greer. She had not asked for the information, indeed, she had not spoken to any of them without them first speaking to her, but he had told her anyway. Often the two younger men would talk to each other of their plans for the money they expected soon. Occasionally they would try to engage the middle-aged man—the one who had hidden himself in her room—in their conversation, but he always refused to take part. Instead he just gazed at the pretty girl with the same lecherous and sickening look he had given her the night he had kidnapped her in her bedroom.

Melissa feared him more than the others; she did not like the gaze he constantly turned upon her. And strange though it was, whenever he leered at her, she would rein up her horse closer to that of the white-haired leader. Somehow she sensed that he would not let harm come to her as long as he was near. She could read that in his mute stare and troubled eyes, and it was the closest thing to comfort she had felt since her capture.

And so today on the third day of the journey Melissa rode alongside the leader's horse, staring silently ahead of her and wondering where she was bound. She longed to reach some destination, if for no other reason than to get some idea of what might happen to her. It was being unsure that drove her crazy and made her want to scream. She refused herself that release, though; she would not lose her dignity, what little was left of it, in front of her captors.

A raucous song erupted behind her. One of the younger men was singing—it sounded like Greer—loud and off-key. He continued for some time, until the gruff voice of the middle-aged man broke him off with a curse. The younger man laughed and taunted the other until the white-haired leader turned in his saddle to quiet the growing conflict.

"Shut up back there. You're more trouble than you're worth, Greer. Leave Moss alone. If he wants to talk to you he will." There was a surprising amount of power in the gravelly voice of the old man.

Melissa glanced back at Greer when the leader was finished, curious about how he would react to the old man's harsh words. She saw anger in the young man's expression, but he said nothing in response. The white-haired man was looking ahead again, and Greer's eyes turned toward Melissa. He grinned in a way that sickened her, and he gestured at the leader beside her and silently mouthed something, most of which Melissa did not catch. One word came through, though: "crazy." Melissa turned away.

Crazy—could that be what was so disturbingly different about the man beside her? Maybe it was a troubled and diseased mind which cast such a strange light into his eyes. Crazy or not, she could tell one thing for certain—the nameless old man was unhappy, even miserable. She could tell that at one glance.

She looked at him again, and he returned her glance only a moment. Yet in that short time she could see again the pain that showed so clearly in his gaze. She looked away, confused and bothered. She wished she could erase that gaze from her mind. But there it stayed, burning into her brain.

It did not depart as they made camp that night, and it was to remain for the other two days of the trip, night and day. She slept little that night, restlessly stirring and gazing at the Colorado stars from her thin bedroll. Matt—where was he? Would he come after her? She closed her eyes and prayed with her deepest feeling that she would again see him, again touch and kiss him. Then she began to cry again, her tears flowing fast and silent sobs wracking her body in the darkness.

ii

Matt chewed on his jerky and wished he had a fire and a hot cup of black coffee. But he knew that he couldn't risk that, not as close as they were to the band of kidnappers. So far they had successfully avoided making them aware of their presence, and that was of paramount importance right now. Fire and hot food and drink would be a luxury. There was nothing to do but sleep and keep watch when his turn came.

He could hear Hopper and Jernigan talking in quiet voices a few yards away. He knew their topic without making out their words; they were discussing the only thing they had talked about since their journey began three days ago: What was the best way to get Melissa back unharmed?

Matt had ceased taking part in the discussions. He sensed that he was too emotionally involved and far too inexperienced in this sort of thing to make any useful contributions to the debate. He preferred to trust the judgment of the two older men. Matt realized the absurdity of the wild desires he felt when he thought of Melissa's rescue. He wanted to bolt into their camp, pump lead into her captors' skulls, and drag Melissa away from them by sheer force.

It would never work. Matt knew that, so he just

kept his mouth shut, forcing reason to win out over his impatient and turbulent emotions. The thing to do now was to trust whatever decision the two more experienced men made.

He lay back on his bedroll, putting his hands behind his head and looking up into the stars shimmering from the black velvet of the nighttime sky. It looked so deep, so vast. Laying on the earth like this always caused Matt to feel insignificant in the gigantic clockwork of the universe. He remembered his mother reading to him from the family Bible in the old homestead back in Kentucky—something about no sparrow falling to earth without God being aware of it. He pondered the thought, turning it over in his mind. Somehow in this terrible situation it was comforting, and he repeated it again and again to himself.

Hopper's voice came drifting along quiet in the evening breeze. "I don't know, Ezra—I've been wonderin' myself if we shouldn't go in and take her right now instead of waitin'. Once she's in that old monastery I don't know how we'll get her out. It's a tough situation either way we go."

"The question is when will they have their guard at the lowest," Jernigan said. "I refuse to make any move that might endanger Melissa if there's a less dangerous way we can do it later on."

Hopper responded, "Of course, they don't know they're bein' followed—it ain't likely they're really expectin' anybody to try to take Melissa from 'em. We could probably surprise 'em right now."

There was a pause, and Matt could tell Jernigan was thinking hard. "Well, I think you're right as far as them guardin' against anyone followin' from the ranch, but that don't necessarily mean their guard is low. There's other men on these plains, not much different than them that took Melissa. And you know as well as I do there's a lot of 'em that would like to get their hands on a pretty young girl like her. Right now she's worth fifty thousand dollars to those kidnappers, and you can bet they're bein' careful with her. They ain't gonna risk losin' her. She's an ace up their sleeve, and I doubt they're bein' too careless with her.''

"So you figure it'll be too risky to try to take her before they reach Beggar's Gulch?''

"Yep. They'll be too much on edge right now.''

"Do you think they'll be any less careful once they get her inside that monastery?''

"Yes, I think they will,'' Jernigan answered. "For one thing, they won't have to worry about some other gang takin' her then. And they don't expect us for a week yet. Once they get inside they'll think their job is finished. I expect it would be a lot easier to surprise 'em.'' He paused. "I just can't risk gettin' Melissa killed by tryin' to take her now.''

Hopper sat quietly in the darkness, considering what he had just heard. Matt listened across the camp for his response.

"It makes sense, Ezra. I reckon you're right.''

"It's settled, then. We'll follow the original plan. We're two days from Beggar's Gulch. We'll make our move as soon as we can after we get there.''

Our move, Matt repeated mentally. What move? He desperately hoped that one of the two men had some plan in mind. To him it seemed they were preparing for nothing less than a ride into hell.

14

A chilling sense of dread crept slowly over Melissa as she rode through the Colorado countryside alongside the leader of her captors. She sensed she was near the end of her journey. She wasn't sure how she knew; maybe it was the increased ease apparent in the riders and the greater carelessness with which they spoke and laughed. It was obvious they were confident that their job had been successful.

They rode at an increased pace, obviously anxious to reach their destination. Where could it be? Melissa's eyes scanned the horizon, looking for some sign of a camp or building. But all she saw was the rolling grasslands broken by occasional rocks and scrubby stands of trees. Farther out before her were more rugged hills, and faint in the western horizon were hazy, snowcapped peaks of blue and purple intruding their rugged promontories into the sky.

She found no indication of where they might be going, yet a feeling of vague apprehension increased with each beat of her horse's hooves on the grassland. She glanced behind her at the other riders. The two younger ones were grinning, Greer especially, and even in Moss's stony face she could see some faint parody of a smile. The sight left her doubtless that very soon she would know what was to become of her.

The terrain grew more rugged as they advanced, and stands of evergreens and aspens occurred more frequently. The hills became sharper and taller, but nothing she saw could prepare her for the breathtaking sight she beheld when the riders steered their horses into a thicket directly before them and halted.

They were atop an immensely high cliff, steep but not sheer, and below them stretched out a vast green plain of low slopes and smooth hills. Occasional large knolls of rock thrust up from the ground in that plain, looking like stones tossed from the cliff by some giant hand into the dirt. The whole scene was a panorama of vastness, and the green of the hills melted into the blue of the sky at the borders of the distant horizon to the south, and in the west those hills grew into the purple and silver of the mountains.

But even the vast magnificence before her could not draw Melissa's attention away from the sight directly below the cliff, which sloped around on each side to form the walls of a large box canyon. Her mouth was slightly open and her breath came faster as she stared down the steep slope to the unbelievable thing hundreds of feet below.

It was a monastery—it could be nothing else. The white stone of the buildings and the wall which extended across the mouth of the canyon had the look of a place of worship. And the white-stone building in the midst of the courtyard could be nothing else but a chapel.

The enclosure below stirred a vague feeling of

recognition in Melissa. She had heard of this place, but she somehow couldn't attach a name to it. Her inability to remember troubled her, but the apprehensive stirrings rising within her troubled her more. Although the monastery had undoubtably been built to glorify God, it now seemed infested with evil.

She had no doubt that they had at last reached their destination. She wondered which building below would become her prison. And in a deeper part of her mind she wondered if once she set foot inside that walled enclosure she would ever leave. Perhaps it would be more than a prison. It could be her death chamber.

Melissa was numb, as if she was becoming calloused in her misery. For a fleeting second she again thought of Matt.

"Well, there it is, men," the leader said. "We're back."

"Then why we sittin' up here?" grumbled Greer. "Let's move on down. I could use a good bowl of stew. This dried meat and beans business is about to get to me. I'm ready for some real food."

The leader clicked his tongue and wheeled his horse around away from the bluff edge. Melissa followed, and the other men fell in behind. They rode silently toward the west, preparing to circle around down the slope to the level of the plain on which the monastery sat. They would come around to it on its west side. The men were totally at ease now, confident that they had delivered their cargo safely. No one could take the girl from them this close to their destination.

Melissa's mind worked rapidly as she rode, trying to attach a name to the place to which they were riding. It was frustrating to be unable to do it. She was sure she had heard of some place like this before—it seemed her father had spoken of it. And if she recalled correctly, what he had said had not been good.

When they reached the base of the hill and began to circle eastward through the stand of trees around the foot of the slope, Melissa remembered. She shuddered as she sounded the name over in her mind, and hope departed. Beggar's Gulch. . . Beggar's Gulch. . .Beggar's Gulch. . . . It played through her mind incessantly like the mocking chant of some demon.

Of all the places she could never imagine actually seeing, this was one of the most unlikely. Beggar's Gulch had always been only a legend to her, an unreal threat used by mothers to quiet naughty children. Her mother had told her many times when she was small that she must be good or find herself carried away to this place. But that had been misty, nebulous—not unbearably real like this.

She had listened many times as her father and his companions had talked of this infamous place and the evil men who had dwelled there through the years. No one dared approach. Its gaping canyon mouth was like a doorway to hell for those who had no business there.

She saw the sentry on the wall grip his rifle tensely as the band of riders moved out from the trees into the open plain in clear view of the wall. He stared hard at them, then relaxed and waved in a gesture of excitement in their direction. He turned and yelled into the enclosure, though it was moments before the echoes of his cry rebounded off the canyon wall to reach the little party of riders: "They're here! They've got the girl!"

Melissa glanced quickly at the men behind her. They were grinning, their mouths open widely and their backs straight and proud in the saddle. Their task was virtually complete; now all they had to do was sit and wait the several days until the ransom arrived. The situation was completely to their liking.

Only the nameless leader was unsmiling. He stared straight ahead, seeming unwilling to look at any of his fellow riders. He appeared confused, disoriented. Melissa suspected that Greer was right when he indicated that the man was insane. It was chilling to think about—being that close to a crazy man. Yet she felt his insanity was preferable to the evil rationality of the others. Again she felt she should remain close to him, that he would be some sort of protection for her. She hated him almost as much as she hated the others, yet he provided something vaguely like comfort to the distressed girl.

The huge door to the enclosure swung open wide to welcome them as they approached, and Melissa hung her head as she rode through the portal. There were only a handful of men inside, yet she felt as if she were being displayed like a side of beef before a huge throng as the inhabitant of the monastery hooted and jeered lewdly at her. She heard the men behind her laugh, but the leader remained cold and stony-faced. He stared at the yelling, grinning group of men and his eyes flashed lightning in their direction.

From his looks, Melissa almost expected him to lunge in fury at her tormentors, but instead they grew rapidly silent. Such was the power and bearing of the white-haired leader that the men quieted under his gaze. It was a singular sight to behold, and in the midst of her humiliation Melissa felt awe.

And her sense of dependence upon the leader increased, too. Yet even then she feared him—feared and despised him as she did all the others. But she knew for certain with the occurrence she had beheld that her suspicion was accurate: As long as the fiery-eyed leader was around she need fear no harm from the others. Whether she was safe from him—well, that was another matter.

The noise from the band of outlaws began to rise again, and a torrent of questions burst forth. Had there been any attempt to stop them when they took the girl? Had they been followed? Would the ransom arrive soon? All of the questions were answered by members of the party, and the inquirers whooped out their satisfaction.

Never had Melissa felt so abused, so belittled. To these men she was not even a human being—she was a ticket to quick and illicit riches. Once their use for her was over, she could expect nothing but death—that is, unless the strange leader forbade it. But even if she should die, she felt she almost wouldn't care. Only the thought of Matt and her family gave her any will to go on. But for the separation from them death would create, it seemed a delicious escape from this devilish existence.

The men dismounted, and Melissa did the same. Immediately her arm was grasped by a fat man in dirty white clothes and she was rudely hustled toward the rear of the enclosure. She said nothing to her rough companion, and his only communication with her was the hungry leer which he aimed toward her. She gasped as she was shoved into a small building built close against the rear slope of the steep cliff upon which they paused some time before. The fat man grunted as he closed the heavy door behind her, cutting off the sunlight.

Melissa blinked in the dim light and looked around her. The room was tiny, and the sole piece of furniture inside was one small bunk. The room was dirty, and in the small shaft of sunlight which streamed in through the single barred window Melissa could see dusty floating in abundance. There was nothing else—no lamp, no chair—nothing.

The room seemed especially miniscule to the girl who had for days now been on the open plains. The walls seemed to rush in toward her, trying to choke her within their dusty embrace. But at least the room was cool, and the darkness was restful to her eyes. Yet she knew that the evening chill would be especially cold within those stone walls.

Melissa crossed her arms in front of her and paced about the room. Outside she could hear the noise and bustle of the men as they unsaddled horses and celebrated their successful mission. At that moment she understood what it was to truly hate, for she loathed and despised them all, from the arrogant young Greer to the crazed white-haired leader.

She threw herself down on the small, dirty bed and lay still. She thought of Matt, her parents. How far they seemed from her now! She yielded herself up to despair.

Outside the men talked, jested, cursed, laughed jubilation over their good fortune and the wealth which they soon expected. Only one was silent—the leader, who stood like a sentinel behind the chapel, his face twisted in disturbed confusion and his lips silently mouthing a single name while he stared at the tiny stone structure which held the lovely prisoner.

15

Greer was silent in the flickering light of the kerosene lamp which sat before him on the rough table. He sipped whiskey from a cracked crockery cup, and his countenance was set in an expression of deep thoughtfulness. Beside him was Jake Benton, the other young man who had accompanied the party of kidnappers. He too was drinking, and his silence was as deep as his partner's.

Most of the other men in the chapel were not so quiet. They were laughing and swearing with abandon, several of them drunken and the others getting that way. The white-haired leader was sitting alone in one corner, sipping his whiskey slowly and pondering something that apparently was bothering him, for his expression was troubled, and he seemed oblivious to the noise around him.

Above the whole scene hung a crucifix with the carved wooden form of the suffering Christ upon it, the agony of death forever fixed on his wooden face. The orgy upon which the sightless eyes gazed was a travesty of the worship for which the chapel had been intended. The incongruity of the whole affair was set off most dramatically by the battered hat which sat irreverently upon the tip of the crucifix's vertical beam.

The usually reserved Moss was loud tonight, bellowing like a bull in his intoxicated state. He was talking proud and haughty about his plans for his share of the ransom money.

"I'll get myself some prime grazin' land, someplace where the law ain't after me, and some good hardy stock. Then I'll go back an' marry that woman I met in Illinois and we'll settle down on that land and raise us a bunch of young'uns. Lord, it'll be grand! I'm sick of this roamin' life—I want to settle down for good. And when that money gets here, I aim to do it!"

No one was listening to him, but it made no difference. He raised his glass to his lips again and drained a quantity of rye that would choke most men, then continued his rambling oration with undisturbed fervor.

A group of the more drunken men were attempting a poker game, the stakes being shares of the ransom they anticipated., They were doing a pretty sorry job of it, their fingers trembling from intoxication. And the constant gripes of one of the gamblers of the chill in the room finally led the group to head outside with the intention of building a fire. After they left, the room was empty but for the leader, the two silent outlaws, and the loud and blustering Moss, who still rambled on in a loud voice to no one in particular.

Greer began clicking the bottom of his cup with a steady rhythm against the table. His thoughts were growing more passionate, if his tightly pursed lips and creased brow were any indication.

"Damn it, Jake, I've been thinkin'. That little gal out there ain't gonna live nohow—there ain't no way none of us are gonna risk lettin' her identify us later on—and it seems a durned shame that she's out there just goin' to waste—you understand what I mean?" He looked at his partner with a gaze full of evil import. "She's mighty pretty, and out here it ain't often a feller gets a chance to be with a woman."

Jake's gaze grew more lecherous. "You know, that's just what I've been thinkin' all this time. I been watchin' her ever since we took her—watchin' and thinkin'. And now I'm ready to do a little more than just thinkin'."

"Well, friend, there ain't no time better than right now!" Greer grinned as he stood, pushing back the empty whiskey cask on which he had been seated. Benton did the same.

Greer swaggered as he walked toward the rear of the chapel and the door which led out in the direction of Melissa's prison. Before he was halfway across the room the white-haired man stood, breaking out of his reverie and becoming suddenly alert.

"Where you boys goin'?"

Benton said nothing but looked a little sheepish. He waited for Greer to respond. Something about the old leader frightened him—it always had. And he knew it was true for most of the other gang members. Only Greer was brash enough to face up to him; even such hardened men as Moss wilted under the leader's gaze.

Greer's face showed derision as he stared back into the bronzed and wrinkled face that frowned down at him. Greer was a head shorter than the other man, but he puffed out his chest and stretched up to his tallest to compensate for it.

"I'm headin' out back. What I do there is my business."

The other man said nothing, but rage burned deep inside him and hung like a threatening aura all around him. Benton grew weak inside, and he wasn't even the target of that piercing stare.

"You mind gettin' outta my way?" Greer's voice was deliberately arrogant and challenging, though Benton imagined it somewhat weaker than before.

"I heard you two talkin' over there. You go near her and I'll kill you." There was no expression in the voice.

Greer's nostrils flared, and his growing anger overpowered the fear that was making his heart pound ever faster. He was getting tired—bone tired —of the domination of this older man, tired of the unquestioned authority he wielded in the gang, tired of the derision he had so often suffered from him. Greer's pride was one of his few possessions, and any man that trod on it was on dangerous ground indeed.

"Move your damn butt, mister. I'll do what I want with no interference from you. The only thing that gal's good for beside the ransom money is—"

The fist that pounded into Greer's face broke not only his nose but every one of his front teeth. Blood squirted out and splattered on the stone tiles of the floor as the young man staggered backward. He felt as if a club had pounded into his face, and he was dazed. He spit out a sickening mixture of fresh blood and broken teeth onto the floor, and stared in pain-wracked fury and shock at the stony-countenanced man before him.

132

"Why you—" Greer's voice was muffled, his missing teeth making clear speech impossible. "Draw." His voice choked off as his right hand flashed toward his hip.

There was no change in the expression of the older man as his hand moved in a blur of speed to his belt, but it was not a gun that he drew from it. Benton couldn't tell what was happening when the leader's hand flashed forward while Greer's gun was only halfway out of its holster. But a moment later Greer was lying on his back on the floor and a large knife was stuck to the hilt in his heart. The young man made several pitiful choking sounds, then his eyes glazed, the expression of incredulity permanently frozen on his open-mouthed face.

Benton stared in shock at the limp body of his comrade, then at the silent form of the man who had just killed him. He could say nothing, only gaze at him in astonished fear, like a rabbit cowering from a rattler.

"Do you want the same treatment?" The words were cold and very sincere.

It took several agonizing attempts before Benton could force his voice from his fear-constricted throat. "No—no sir, I—please, I'll give you no trouble." Benton raised his hands high in the air in a gesture of non-aggression and backed away.

"Move your filthy hide outta my sight." It took Benton only moments to obey, darting across the chapel and out the front door.

The old man watched him leave, then walked over to the body of his victim. He pulled the knife from the motionless chest and cleaned it on Greer's shirt before placing it again in its sheath. Then he turned and walked through the back door into the night.

Only the wooden eyes of the carved Messiah continued to gaze upon the dead body of Greer. And Moss sat alone at the table, still espousing his plans to the empty room, unaware of any of the events that had just transpired.

16

Matt, Jernigan, and Hopper sat like mounted statues upon the brink of the cliff high above Beggar's Gulch. They were obscured from view from the canyon by the scrubby stand of aspens which lined the canyon rim, but through the leaves they could see the stone structure below, well-protected by the steep canyon walls.

The fortress-like structure had a Spanish look, its former function as a monastery clearly evident from the brown stone chapel which stood in prominence in the midst of the dusty courtyard. But no longer was it an instrument of God; the devil had control of the monastery and its inhabitants now. The men who dwelled in the former home of men of prayer had only one god—gold. And there was nothing they would not do to get it. Somewhere in that rathole, Matt thought grimly, was Melissa. What might have become of her even now, in the hands of men so cruel and heartless that nothing could stand in the way of their self-gratification?

"We were blasted fools to ride out on the cliff-edge like this," Hopper said. "This would be a likely spot for a lookout."

"I reckon you got a point, Hopper," Jernigan responded. "It's a good thing for us that they didn't put a man up here—we would have botched things for sure ridin' out like a Fourth of July parade like this." He paused, thinking. "It makes me wonder, though—they must be low on men, else they would have posted a guard up here, it seems."

"Surely them five horses we been trailin' ain't the whole bunch of em!" exclaimed Hopper. "Countin' one horse for Melissa, that would leave only four of 'em!"

"It's likely a few remained behind, I guess," said Jernigan. "Somebody had to hold down the fort, so to speak. Still, there might by only a handful in all—whoa, now! Take a look."

Down below the trio could see a hefty man coming out of the back of the chapel, carrying something in front of him. It was too far away for Matt to tell for sure, but it looked like a tray with food. The man carried it to one of the smaller buildings at the rear of the enclosure, built almost up against the base of the cliff. He balanced the tray on one hand as he unlocked the door, then entered to return moments later, empty-handed.

"That's where they're keepin' Melissa for sure!" Matt exclaimed. "That fellow was takin' victuals to her—it must mean that she's all right."

"Lord, I hope so, son," Jernigan said. "I don't know who else they would be keepin' locked away like that, unless they got prisoners we don't know about."

"There's nothin' to do 'til night comes," said Hopper. "I figure the best thing for us to do right

136

now would be to make camp somewhere a good ways from this rise and get some rest, then make our move come nightfall.''

The idea was agreeable to the other two, so the trio moved away from the cliff edge and headed back into the rolling hills behind them. Matt felt a stirring restlessness inside him. It was hard to be this close to Melissa and the scoundrels who had taken her and not be able to move. But he knew Hopper was right—there was nothing to do but wait out the day, and a long day it promised to be. At least it was past noon; they wouldn't have to wait out the morning too.

It was in a well-hidden draw far back from the cliff edge that the three riders made camp. There was no fire. Although the outlaws' refuge was far below them, hidden from sight by the bluff, they could take no chance at being seen, no matter how remote.

Matt had first watch; he figured he was too keyed up to sleep, anyway. He sat with his knees drawn up in front of him on the little ridge on the side of the draw, and in his mind were pictures of Melissa as he remembered her last—her long brown hair shining in the sun, her long skirts bunched up to her knees, and her lovely mouth open in laughter as she waded through the waters of Walker's Creek back at the Jernigan ranch. Sitting there in the bright Colorado sunshine, Matt realized how deeply he loved the daughter of Ezra Jernigan, and how important it was that she be recovered safely from her captors. That was the only thing in life worth living for—getting Melissa back as soon as possible.

And as for the men who had taken her, well, he intended to see them pay, and pay dearly. Not since that terrible day six years before in Briar Creek had

Matt felt the desire for revenge flow through his system with such awful force. He intended to avenge himself upon her captors, no matter what the cost to himself and no matter how many there were. His hand tightened against the stock of his rifle and his face hardened in determination. Soon, very soon, he intended to free his captured lover and destroy her kidnappers, or lay dead on the earth for his effort.

Matt remained at his post long past the appointed time for him to wake Hopper. It wasn't until the wire-thin cowpoke finally awoke on his own and replaced Matt that the young man finally headed to his bedroll, where he dropped quickly into a fitful, light slumber, the sounds of gunfire and images of conflict rolling through his dreams.

The western sky was barely aglow with the last remnants of sunset when Matt felt Jernigan shake him awake. The pair said not a word to each other but gathered up their bedrolls in the fading light and mentally preparing themselves for what was to come. It wasn't a time for talk. After the camp had been cleaned up, the pair joined Hopper as he saddled up his horse. They did the same, then mounted.

Jernigan spoke. "I figure the best thing we can do is head back to the spot where we were yesterday, and take a good look again. Then we can figure out some sort of plan. It ain't gonna be easy to get into that enclosure, and I think the clearer our plans are, the better it'll be for us."

"You reckon they might have a lookout posted since we left?"

"It's possible, but I doubt it," replied Jernigan. "Still, let's keep an extra sharp lookout in case they have. No shootin' unless absolutely necessary, though—that would warn 'em down below that someone's up here.''

As the three riders approached the canyon rim, their eyes studied every bush, tree, and rock that might hide a lookout. But there was no one in sight, and by the time they reached the cliff edge, they were satisfied that they were alone.

The enclosure below would have been nearly invisible but for the faint moonlight which shimmered hazily across the prairie in intermittent bursts between the clouds which floated across the dark sky and the fire apparently just being built on the west side of the chapel. There was a faint glow of coal-oil lamps from the windows of the chapel and the structures on the east side of the enclosure. Each individual point of light was just a dim candle-flicker from high above, scarcely visible for the most part. Occasional dark shadows flitted across the growing bonfire, indicating that men were moving about in the courtyard.

"They've got a sentry on the front wall," Hopper pointed out.

"I see him," said Jernigan. "I figure just as much. He's gonna be a problem when it comes to trying to get inside that wall. It cuts off our angle of approach, too. It looks to me like we'll have to come around from the west if we're gonna get the drop on 'em at all. You see that stand of timber over yonder along the west edge of the canyon mouth? That'll hide us when we come around. After that I ain't sure what we can do."

"Let's head on down that way," Matt suggested. "Maybe from that angle we can figure out the best way."

The three riders reined their horses around and headed back from the canyon rim. Once they had cleared the scrubby aspens, they headed west to make the long circle around and down to the level of the plain fronting the box canyon. They said little, each trying to visualize the best way they could get past that sentry and into the walled monastery. But after they were in, how would they escape the notice of the men around the fire? And what would they do if they were wrong in their guess as to the numbers of the gang? Matt was getting doubtful about whether or not they should have set out on such a mission with only three men. But then again, how would a large group have preserved the element of secrecy and surprise that was going to be necesssary if they were to rescue Melissa alive?

The ride took close to an hour, since the downward progress made the travel difficult for the horses, and the darkness made the trail nearly invisible. But after the descent from the high ground above the canyon was completed, the ground leveled out suddenly and progress became much easier. It wasn't long before the trio was hidden in the stand of aspens that from the canyon rim had appeared as so much grass. The moon broke through a bank of clouds, illuminating the canyon suddenly and shining across the land in front of it. The sentry would have a clear view should they try to break through the trees right now and make for the enclosure.

"Hopper, what do you think?" Jernigan asked.

The lanky cowboy rubbed his chin in his calloused hand as he studied the moonlit expanse of land before him. Matt could tell that he was formulating a plan in his mind, and for the sake of all of them he hoped it was a good one.

"It seems to me we ain't gonna get nowhere 'til we get that guard off'n the wall yonder," Hopper said. "Trouble is, we can't shoot him without gettin' the whole lot of 'em out here on us. Only way I can figure is for one of us to rope him and drag him off before he can holler and hope nobody notices. And seein' as how I got more experience with a rope than either one of you—not tryin' to brag or nothin', you understand—I think it should be me. The main problem is gettin' across there without bein' spotted."

The cowboy looked at the other two, studying their expressions. Apparently they didn't convince him that his friends were confident about his plan, for after a pause he said rather defensively, "Look, fellers, I know it's wild, but can either of you think of any other way?"

Jernigan's face clouded in thought. "Hopper, I believe you've got the only feasible idea at all. But once we get him off that wall, the ones around that fire are bound to notice sooner or later that he's gone." He looked at Matt in such a way that apprehension prickled up and down the young man's spine.

"Matt, that sentry appears to be about your size. If Hopper can get a rope around his neck and yank him off there before he can warn the others, would you be willin' to put on his clothes and take his place up there? It would be risky, I know, but I don't know what else we could do, and it would be a real ace up our sleeve to have you up there to kinda look things over. As long as you stayed quiet up there, me and Hopper could get across the courtyard without bein' spotted."

Matt waited a long time before answering, trying to think of some other way. But nothing came to mind, so after a pause he turned and looked at Jernigan and said, "I reckon that's the best plan we can come up with. That way even if you're spotted I could probably pick off two or three of them in the courtyard before they could figure where the shootin' was comin' from. I'll do it."

Hopper and Jernigan said nothing. The latter slapped his calloused hand on Matt's shoulder in a gesture which said he understood the courage involved in Matt's decision.

"I'm wonderin' about one thing, though," Matt said. "They're bound to have their sentry duty staggered into shifts. What am I supposed to do if somebody comes out there to replace me? That would sure be the end for all of us."

Jernigan whistled low in perplexity. He hadn't thought of that possibility.

"The way I see it it'll be a risk we'll have to take. One thing I've always noticed 'bout folks on look-out duty—it ain't often that a replacement comes without the fellow already on duty goin' to get him. Just maybe the next man on the shift will sleep right through his time and not come out at all. That's an awful thin limb to stand on, I know, but then nobody ever said this was goin' to be easy —or safe." He looked again at Matt. "But it's your neck that's gonna be on the line out there, Matt. If you don't want to do it, if you want to try it some other way, then there won't be no hard feelin's."

That was it. It was up to Matt now. A million wild schemes flashed through his brain in an instant, only to be rejected as ridiculous. Hopper's plan was the only one. It would probably get them all killed just as quick as any of Matt's schemes, but it stood the best chance of working.

"No, I reckon I won't back out now. We've got to get Melissa outta there someway or other. Hopper, if you can get that sentry off the wall, I'll take his place."

"I knew we could count on you, Matt," grinned Jernigan. His countenance grew cold again, though, as he looked back across the prairie which was still flooded with moonlight.

Hopper was looking at the sky. "Fellers, it looks like that big cloud there is gonna hit the moon. When it does, I'm gonna scamper on across there before that sentry's eyes adjust to the dark. It ain't much of a chance, but it's all I'm gonna get."

"We'll go together, Hopper," said Jernigan. "I ain't lettin' you go out there alone. After all, it's my daughter we're goin' after." Hopper looked like he wanted to argue, but right then the moon slid behind the cloud and immersed the prairie in darkness as deep as that inside a cave. There was the noise of hands slapping pockets, making sure they were well-stuffed with extra cartridges, and the short, quick breathing of men about to make the most important run of their lives.

Hopper scrambled to his horse and loosed his rope from the saddle, and then they were off, running at a trot across the grassland, each trying to make as little noise as possible. It seemed impossible that the sentry would not see them, and Matt expected any second to hear a shout and the roar of gunfire. But it never came. They reached the wall in safety and hugged themselves to it almost directly under the spot the sentry stood.

Matt's mind scurried from one thought to another like a field mouse evading a night owl. He was painfully aware that his performance in the next few minutes would make the difference as to whether he would see Melissa alive again. It was a hard spot to be in.

Hopper's spot was certainly no easier, Matt realized. Everything depended upon the absolute accuracy of his throw and the slim chance that the men inside the enclosure would not notice when the sentry was pulled from the wall, hopefully with as little noise as possible.

Matt knew that it was not because of the darkness that the sentry had not seen them, for before he was halfway to the wall Matt's eyes had adjusted to the darkness, and he had felt perilously exposed. Obviously the fellow just wasn't looking; the poker game around the fire was probably more interesting, and certainly no one inside that wall actually expected anyone to be approaching the dreaded Beggar's Gulch monastery this time of night. Lucky for us, Matt said to himself. It seemed a miracle that they had made it this far.

But even as Hopper began the slow, silent spin of his rope, Matt knew it would take more than one miracle to get them through this night and to bring Melissa safely home. He tried not to breath as the skinny cowboy spun his loop in ever-faster circles, trying to prepare for the critical toss as well as to avoid observation from the sentry, whose back was turned but whose ears would pick up any stray noise the cowboy might produce. It was a tight spot, for sure.

The sentry was in a careless mood, absolutely

sure that the plain behind him was empty. His duties were simply for show, he was certain; there were no threats against the band of outlaws and their roost here in the monastery tonight. He flipped away the stub of his hand-rolled cigarette just as a whirling, faintly whistling something passed quickly downward across his line of vision and clamped with shocking force around his throat.

He had neither the time nor the ability to cry out as he felt himself being jerked from the wall with tremendous force, choking from the vise-like thing constricted around his throat. It made no sense— surely this was not happening! But just before he struck the ground with a choking grunt and a pistol bashed hard against the back of his skull, he knew that it really was.

Jernigan breathed a faint sigh of relief as he stood over the man his pistol had just rendered unconscious. The first part of the ordeal was passed; one portion of this impossible quest was completed. That is—unless the sudden disappearance of the sentry was noticed by those inside the wall.

"Matt, get on this feller's clothes as fast as you can," Jernigan said in a whisper. "We'll hoist you up on the wall as soon as you've changed."

Matt struggled with the outlaw's clothes, his haste making his progress all the slower. But eventually he was dressed in the pants, shirt, and vest of the fallen man, noting with displeasure the foul, sweaty odor of the clothes. Lord! This fellow was a filthy one!

It was not the time to worry about niceties, however lacking they might be, and after Matt had donned the man's hat, which was a shade too large and saw low on his forehead, he looked at Jernigan to signal that he was ready to make the climb up onto the wall. He realized clearly, though he tried to shut out the thought, that when his head peered over the wall, he might be face-to-face with the front end of a rifle, should the men inside have noticed the strange disappearance of the guard.

"That was a good throw, Hopper," Matt whispered as his partners bent down to lift him by his ankles to where he could reach the top of the wall.

"Try to be quiet when you pull yourself up, Matt," came Hopper's voice. "We'll hand your rifle up to you once you get up there."

Matt poked his head slowly up and peeked into the courtyard, trying to keep his head as low as possible. He wouldn't have been surprised if a slug had come whizzing along right then to carry away the top of his skull.

No such thing happened and Matt pulled himself up onto the wall, trying to make as little noise as possible. He was grateful to hear the wail of a mouth harp coming from the direction of the bonfire. Perhaps the sound, though faint to him, might be loud enough to mask any noise he might make. And best of all, it was proof that the gamblers had not noticed the disappearance of their comrade from the wall.

Matt accepted his rifle from Hopper after he had made it to the top of the wall, then he stood up straight, trying to assume the same posture as the previous sentinel. He was in clear view of the courtyard now, and he hoped that he looked enough like the other fellow to fool anyone who might glance in his direction.

Now Hopper and Jernigan were freer to move about outside the wall; there was no one but Matt to see them. Hopper tied up and gagged the unconscious sentry. Judging from the hard lick Jernigan had dealt the man, it was not likely that he would come around for a good while. When he did, he would certainly have a mystery to solve, trying to figure out why he was laying bound on the dirt outside the monastery, gagged and wearing only his longjohns.

As Matt stood quietly upon the wall, he realized that it might be a long wait before they made their next move—whatever that might be. Hopper and Jernigan certainly couldn't clamber over the wall until the men around the fire had finished their poker game, and that could be on up toward morning. It was between ten and eleven now, so it might be a long session of sentry duty that awaited him. Again he hoped that whoever was supposed to replace him later would conveniently sleep through or neglect his obligation. It would be trouble for sure if someone came out here.

So Matt passed his time on the wall in troubled contemplations and desperate attempts to formulate some sort of sensible plan for the rest of their mission. He was unsuccessful, so after a time he gave up and tried to think of nothing in particular. And try as he would, he could not keep himself from stealing long and furtive glances toward the rear of the enclosure and the buildings that lined the cliff base. In one of those dark chambers she was being held—the girl for whom he might well die tonight.

17

Melissa couldn't sleep. The hard cot in her stone prison wouldn't let her relax, but she realized that in her situation no bed would be soft enough to induce sleep. Ever since she had been taken by the band of human scum outside, despair had been a constant companion, her only companion. It had settled into her mind like a fog and refused to clear, and it had robbed her almost entirely of rest.

She longed to see her mother and father, to lie down again in her bed at the ranch, and most of all to see Matt. How she ached to hold him and talk to him again! Where was he now? Was he as despairing as she since the terrible event that had taken her from him? She was sure that he was.

Try as she would, she could not hold back the tears. They coursed down her cheeks freely, and she wept aloud in the darkness. Never before had she experienced such a deep sadness, such a doubt about whether she would live to see the next day—or the next hour. Death could come at any time, at the whim of her captors, even if her father did pay the huge ransom they were demanding. Her father—she wondered if she would ever see him again, or her mother—or Matt.

She could no longer stand to remain in her bed. She arose, straightening the dress she had worn for days now, then walked across her chamber to the one tiny window in the front wall. Flat metal bars crisscrossed over the window, making escape impossible.

She leaned against the window and looked across the dusty courtyard toward the huge front wall. The stone chapel loomed huge before her. It was late; midnight had passed two or three hours ago, and it would not be very long until dawn.

In the center of the yard a bonfire was dying away, and several figures were loitering around it, talking quietly. They stayed for awhile, looking like black wraiths tinged with red from the fading blaze. One of the men stretched his arms above his head as if he were yawning, then the men slowly sauntered toward the large stone building across the east side of the enclosure that served as sleeping quarters for the outlaws. The courtyard was empty now, save for the lone sentry that stood upon the wall, his slightly slumping figure barely visible against the starlit sky. The clouds were gone now, and the black sky was like a piece of sparkling, jeweled velvet.

What was it about the sentry that made Melissa crease her brow and look harder at him? She was mystified, but something in the stance and look of the figure seemed vaguely familiar. For some unaccountable reason her heart begasn to beat faster, and something like hope stirred in the back of her mind.

Yet she felt disturbed too. Why should the still figure of the sentry arouse such a feeling in her? He was one of them—one of the ones who had taken her. Perhaps she was losing her mind; perhaps the pressure and despair was finally getting to be too much. Even if she should live through this ordeal, what would she be when it was all over? It was hard to think about.

She turned away from the window, not noticing the two figures that scrambled up onto the wall beside the sentry and dropped into the darkness of the courtyard, Winchesters in their hands. Still the sentry stood silent, his casual pose unchanged.

There was the sound of boots against the earth, coming toward her chamber. Melissa's breath came faster, and her hand pressed over her heart to still the sudden fearful beating of it. She backed away from the thick oak door as the sound of a key in the lock rattled in the stillness of the tiny room.

As quickly as the door was open she recognized him. It was the leader—she could tell in spite of the darkness that obscured his features. She couldn't see his eyes, but she knew that they burned with the same strange fire that she had noticed before. It was a fire that had grown every time she had seen him, and it frightened her.

"Amanda?" There was a childish, pitiful quality in the gravelly voice that sounded the name.

"I'm not Amanda—I'm Melissa Jernigan. You know that. What do you want?"

The figure moved a little closer and stretched an arm toward her. "Don't tease me, Amanda. You've come again at last—it's been so long. God! I've missed you!"

Melissa's fright was steadily increasing. There was something wrong in the voice, something abnormal and disturbed. She backed away a little further.

"Mister, I don't even know your name, but you

know that I'm Melissa Jernigan. You took me—you're the one that's leading this little band of trash. I'm not your Amanda, whoever she is, so go away, you sickening—"

The inhuman sob that rang out in the darkness was so startlingly unexpected that Melissa backed away until her back touched the cold stone wall at the rear of the room. The man before her was weeping, loudly and pitifully, and he sank to his knees on the stone-tiled floor, his face buried in his hands. He babbled words that she could not make out, and her instincts told her that this was a totally insane man, completely devoid of any connection with reality.

"Amanda—oh, please don't come back only to taunt me! Don't you remember how it was, how we used to love each other? You're just as you were then, so young and pretty. I know I'm older now, Amanda, and I've been sick, very, very sick—but it don't matter now. We can be together again, just like it used to be. I'll take you away from here. I'll keep the others from hurting you—kill them if I have to. Oh, please don't torment me. I've waited so long for you to come back, Amanda!"

In spite of her fear, Melissa felt a sudden and overwhelming burst of pity for the poor creature who knelt before her, weeping like a lost infant for its mother. It was obvious that he identified her as someone he had loved long ago—perhaps even a wife—and she suspected that nothing now could persuade him of her true identity. The growing fire she had seen in the old man's eyes was indeed the light of insanity, an insanity that apparently had grown to fruition only in the past few days.

She stood in uncomfortable silence over the

kneeling, sobbing man, her back against the wall and her hands pressed against the stone on either side of her. In spite of the coolness of the rock, her palms were wet with perspiration. She looked at the man in wordless despair, then glanced out across the courtyard through the open door behind him.

The door—the door was still open! In only a second she realized her opportunity, and in that same second she took advantage of it. She dodged quickly past the weeping man and darted like a cat from her prison. Her feet kicked up little clouds of dust as she ran for the back of the chapel, realizing that she must not be spotted by the sentry. She glanced behind her and into her former prison. The noise of weeping was still audible from within, and it looked as if the man had prostrated himself on the floor in his anguish. Melissa doubted that he realized that she was no longer with him.

But now where could she go? She must remain silent, she realized, so as to not awaken any of the monastery's sleeping inhabitants, and also so she would not catch the attention of the sentry. She realized it would probably be only moments before the crazed man in her cell realized she was gone. Then it would be too late, and her chance would have disappeared.

Panic almost overwhelmed her as she debated what to do. Was there any place she could hide, any corner where she could conceal herself? She could think of nothing. Even if she hid, how could she escape from the high wall of the monastery? She was helpless.

It was panic and not reason that led her to bolt from her position and run toward the east end of the enclosure. And it was total shock and fear that kept her from crying out when she ran full-force into the arms of a tall man that stepped into her path from the side of the chapel.

Her head swam and she felt she would faint as she collapsed into the man's arms. Before blackness engulfed her, she looked with fear-crazed eyes into the face of the figure.

"Hopper!" It was like a whispered cry when she said it, and immediately afterward she collapsed senseless and fainting in the arms of the skinny ranch foreman.

"My God, is she all right?" Jernigan whispered desperately.

"Yeah—she's only fainted, I believe, and I can't rightly blame her. Lord, ain't this a stroke of luck! I don't know how she got out, but right now I ain't gonna try to find out. I'll carry her over to the wall and Matt can pull her up."

Hopper scooped the senseless girl into his arms and joined Jernigan in a desperate dash across the courtyard toward the front wall. Matt was still on the wall, and when he saw the pair coming with Melissa he almost cried out, halfway in joy to see her again and halfway in fear that she was hurt. But he had no time for questions as the men came up below him to the wall, for at that moment there rang across the enclosure a frightening voice that echoed from the walls of the canyon high above the stone monastery.

"Amanda!"

18

i

"That fixes us, for sure," Hopper said in disgust.

Even as Matt hoisted Melissa's unconscious body up to the top of the wall, he could see movement in the sleeping quarters of the outlaws. Hopper clambered up on the wall just as a light appeared faintly in a window. The shout had roused the entire bunch of them, Matt figured.

"Get down on the outside, Matt!" Hopper cried. "I'll let Melissa down to you!"

Matt did as he was told, though somewhat reluctantly. He knew that in a moment men would come out shooting, and it seemed unfair for him to be safe on the outside of the wall while Jernigan and Hopper were clear targets for the outlaws. He wanted to stay and help fight, but he realized that Melissa's welfare came before anything else.

He jumped Indian-like from the wall, his Winchester gripped in both hands. He landed in the dirt and rolled, jumping up immediately and setting the rifle on the ground. He extended up his arms and took Melissa from Hopper just as the sound of shots came from the east end of the enclosure.

"Take her and run for the horses, Matt!" Hopper instructed hurriedly. Matt saw Hopper turn to pull Jernigan up after him, but shots rang out, whizzing through the air to splat against the inside of the wall. A chunk of Hopper's hat went flying as a bullet missed his head by inches, and as Matt turned to carry away Melissa, he saw the cowboy leap down inside the enclosure.

As he ran as fast as he could toward the stand of trees, Matt wondered why Hopper had leaped inside instead of out. It was an almost sure-death move. It took only a moment, though, for him to realize that Hopper was simply refusing to leave Jernigan to fight off the gunmen alone. Jernigan had been unable to make it to the top of the wall before the shooting began, so Hopper had chosen to join rather than desert him. It was a brave deed, Matt knew, for the odds for survival were slim. Matt made for the trees at top speed.

Melissa was beginning to revive as Matt put her down on a soft mound of leaves as he reached the aspen stand. The horses were only a few feet away. The sound of gunfire was continuing from within the monastery, and occasionally a bullet would whine its course far over their heads, or rip through the treetops. In a way, Matt was glad to hear the battle continuing, for it indicated that his two companions were still alive and fighting.

Melissa was dirty and dishevelled in the moonlight as she began to stir awake, but Matt thought he had never seen a prettier sight. Now that she was free, he intended to never let the men who had kidnapped her lay a hand on her again, no

155

matter what it took. He prayed a fervent prayer of thanks that she was uninjured.

"Melissa?"

"Oh—where am I? What's happened to me?" Her words were faint and she appeared disoriented, but it was a relief to Matt to hear her speak.

"It's me, Melissa—Matt. You're safe now. We've rescued you."

Melissa appeared totally disconcerted for a moment as she opened her eyes and stared into Matt's face, her mouth open and in an expression of confusion. Then the tears began, and she reached up and wrapped her arms around Matt's neck and pulled him close to her.

"Oh, Matt, I thought I would never see you again! Has this all been a dream? It seems so confusing and strange—but oh, I'm so glad to see you!"

Matt was almost in tears himself as he hugged the pretty, dark-haired girl to his chest.

"No, Melissa, it wasn't a dream. But it's all over now," he said. "There's something I've got to do. I don't have time to explain, but I want you to do something for me—all right?"

Melissa nodded, her eyes growing clearer as her mind became less foggy.

"Over there is my horse, the roan. I want you to get on it and ride around this stand of trees and circle northwest until you reach the top of the gorge above the canyon. Got it? Wait there for a little while and watch the enclosure. The moonlight's bright enough for you to see. If you see me, Hopper, or your father riding out, wait on us. But if it's someone else, or there's anybody followin' us, take off and keep runnin'. I don't know when we'll be comin' after you, so just be patient. Now I've got to go. I'll—I'll see you later.''

Melissa started to question the young man kneeling beside her, but he crushed her to him suddenly and kissed her lips long and hard. Then he was gone, running away from her, out of the trees, through the moonlight, and back toward the prominent stone wall of the monastery. It was not until then she noticed the sound of gunfire, and a vague understanding of what was happening began to dawn in her mind.

Matt had said that her father and Hopper were here. . .now she remembered! It was Hopper who she had run into inside the wall. It was his face she had seen before she lapsed into a faint. It made sense now—her father, Matt, and Hopper had come after her, to take her from her captors. Now they were fighting for their lives within the wall, and Matt had returned to join them.

She had been told to run, but she knew that she could not, not while three brave men were risking their lives for her sake. She stood under the trees and brushed the dirt and leaves from her dress. Her mind was working fast—what could she do to help in the fight? She turned and noticed the horses, then a sudden idea struck her.

Melissa ran over the the three tethered animals and began rifling through the saddlebags on her father's horse. She smiled as her hand found what she sought. She was no longer helpless.

ii

Jernigan wiped sweat from his brow as he bent over his hot Winchester and continued pumping

157

shots toward the windows of the chapel where the outlaws had taken refuge. Hopper was hunkering down beside him, reloading. Both men were grateful for the large number of shells they had loaded into their pockets, though even that number would not be enough to hold out long against the better-equipped men they were fighting.

The pair had holed up in the first place they could reach, a stone building similar to the one Melissa had been held in but with more windows. It appeared to have been designed as some sort of sleeping chamber originally, though now it was apparently used for storage, for there were crates and boxes stacked high around the walls. Though the darkness made it hard to see, the place seemed filthy and cobwebs hung thick from the ceiling.

Bullets smacked into the walls and the crates and barrels stacked all around them. Jernigan's eye squinted as he leveled his sights on a man who was trying to scamper from the outlaws' sleeping quarters to the chapel to join the rest of the gunmen. Just as the man started to leap through the open chapel door, Jernigan squeezed the trigger and the slug caught the man in the side, knocking him back dead on the dirt.

"There's one less to worry about," Jernigan muttered as he ducked his head down inside to reload his now-empty rifle.

Hopper took his place at the window, squeezing off a shot before asking, "How many of 'em do you figure, Ezra?"

"I don't know, Hopper. I would guess seven or eight. I can't be sure, though—didn't take the time to count 'em."

A bullet whizzed by Hopper's head and ripped

through a box behind him, causing him to duck down with a startled look on his face. He whistled and shook his head, then again thrust his rifle barrel out the window to begin firing. In the east the first rays of dawn were beginning to glow.

He fired at a head that popped up in one of the chapel windows, but from the sudden spray of crushed stone that exploded from the sill he knew he had missed. The head ducked down, then reappeared over the barrel of a rifle, and Hopper began to squeeze down again.

A split second before he fired, the head jerked suddenly, then disappeared as if it had been struck by a shot. But whose shot? He hadn't even fired yet when it struck. The cowpoke turned to glance at the front wall just in time to see Matt jump down inside the courtyard, his rifle in his hand, and run toward the storage area where he and Jernigan were holed up. The dust around Matt's running feet kicked up where slugs were striking, but still he continued at a fast trot, dodging to make himself a more elusive target in the dim early-morning light.

"Why, that blasted fool!" Hopper exclaimed. "He'll get himself killed for sure! I told him to tend to Melissa and leave us to fight these devils! The little bull-headed shorthorn!"

Jernigan jumped in surprise when something big and dark lunged through the open window in a dive and landed in a heap on the floor. It was Matt, who in his haste had decided that the most direct entrance to the storage house—the window—was preferable to the farther-away door.

"You damn fool, I told you to stay with Melissa!" Hopper shouted as Matt picked himself up.

"She's all right—I made sure of that," Matt responded. "But if you think I'm gonna run off and leave you to fight no tellin' how many gunmen without my help, you got another thing comin'! Now don't argue with me!"

Hopper's mouth fell open in surprise at the forceful words of the young man. He started to shout back angrily, but instead his homely face twisted into a smile and he said, "Well, I reckon you got more grit than I figured."

"In case you two have forgotten, we've got a gun battle goin' on," Jernigan growled. "Get to shootin' but don't waste ammunition."

"I got some extra cartridges in my pockets," Matt said. "And I guess we'll need 'em."

There came a tremendous burst of gunfire from the chapel then, and all three of the cornered men had to duck their heads to avoid being struck by flying lead. It seemed the outlaws were hoping that a sudden blitz of fire would end the fight.

Instead they got a return blitz from the storage area, with Matt adding his own fire from the slightly open door while Jernigan and Hopper continued their volley from the window. Matt wasn't certain, but he thought he winged one of the gunmen.

As he reloaded his hot and smoking Winchester, he glanced toward the small building which had been Melissa's prison. In the doorway stood a man, no gun or weapon in his hand, looking blankly across the courtyard. Matt stared hard; something in the man's stance reminded him of someone, his father perhaps. He had no time to contemplate the man, but he wondered who he was and why he stood so dangerously exposed to a stray shot.

Two shots blasted dirt up into his face, and Matt pulled his head quickly back from the door. He finished reloading his rifle and shifted back toward his firing position.

The bullets continued to whine through the air from the chapel, but consistently they shot high. Matt thought it was just bad shooting, but the shots continued to whip past the heads of the three men and smack into the rear wall without even coming close to them. Matt twisted his head around to look behind him, and what he saw froze his blood and told him why the men in the chapel were firing as they were.

Sitting on top of a barrel was a wooden crate. One corner had been torn off by a shot, and through the splintered hole Matt could clearly see something which made him feel even less safe than he had before.

It was dynamite—from the looks of things a full crate of it. Had the shot come a quarter of an inch closer, the entire west side of the enclosure would have been blown almost halfway up the canyon wall, with Matt, Jernigan, and Hopper right along with it.

"Mr. Jernigan, take a look at that!" Matt exclaimed when he found his voice.

Jernigan had other things on his mind at the moment, but the furtive tone of Matt's voice cause him to take notice. He followed the young man's gaze to the wooden box, then let out a low whistle that bespoke his awe.

"Well, I wonder what that's doing here!" he

exclaimed. "Likely as not they've got it stored up to blow some safe somewhere. Or it could have been here a long time before this bunch got here. But not matter where it came from, they're sure 'nough shootin' for it. They're tryin' to blow us clean outta the state!"

"We gotta move it quick," Hopper said.

Matt sat his rifle against the wall and crawled over to where Jernigan was crouched. He and the gray-haired rancher moved slowly toward the rear of the room, conscious of the whizzing bullets pouring in ever-increasing numbers from the chapel. And the shots were getting closer and closer to the threatening box of dynamite.

Matt knew the minute he and Jernigan raised up to lift the box from its resting place they would be in clear view of the chapel and an easy target for the gunmen. But it was a risk they would have to take. The risk involved in leaving the dynamite where it was was far greater.

The old box creaked as they lifted it from the barrel. A bullet whizzed between the two men only a foot or so above the crate. Matt jerked slightly—a move that brought him a reproving glance from Jernigan. He didn't have to be told how important it was to move slowly and carefully right now, but the bullets flying around him made it hard to do.

Hopper was still shooting, but over the noise of his rifle he said, "Take it easy, men. I always wanted to go out in a blaze of glory, but that ain't what I had in mind."

The two men tried to keep their heads low as they inched toward the front of the room, bringing the dynamite out of line with the path of the hot, singing lead from the chapel. As soon as the dynamite was safe they sat it down, breathing in relief and pulling their heads out of target range.

Jernigan picked up his rifle and joined Hopper at the window. He let fly a long volley of lead, his rifle blazing and smoking from the burst of fire. The acrid smell of burning gunpowder was in the air, and noise of rifle fire was deafening. Even more deafening, Matt thought, would be the roar of that dynamite should anything set it off.

Jernigan pulled back from the window after his long burst of fire. He set his rifle aside and pulled a cigar stub from his pocket and thrust it between his teeth. He struck a match and lit the stub, puffing it until its tip glowed red. Smoke billowed from his nostrils as he carefully lifted the lid of the crate. Matt realized suddenly what he had in mind.

Matt estimated that there must be fifty or sixty sticks in the crate, each one looking deadly. The dynamite was old, which only made it more dangerous. The fuses were still intact, though, and Jernigan selected a stick with a very long one from the bunch at the top. He lifted it carefully, then shifted his position so he would be clear to toss it through the window.

"Men, when I light this thing, hit the floor!" he commanded as he touched the burning tip of his cigar stub to the fuse.

The fuse flared more quickly than any of them thought it would, and Matt caught his breath as the fuse rapidly shortened. Before it burned completely down Jernigan tossed the stick toward the chapel wall.

It fell short, but the concussion from the deafening blast had an effect nonetheless. Matt heard the cries of frightened and injured men as the blast echoed up the walls of Beggar's Gulch. Dust and grit flew everywhere in the courtyard, and the walls of the chapel cracked and sent down a shower of stone chips and shattered mortar. There was no serious damage, but Matt knew that the odds had turned in their favor now—and their enemies knew it too.

Matt rolled back to his position at the doorway and thrust his rifle barrel outside. He saw a hefty man—he guessed the same one he had seen earlier carrying food to Melissa—stagger out of the chapel doorway, yelling horribly and gripping his face. The blast had apparently thrown rock into his eyes with the force of a scattergun. He was blinded, and a pitiful sight he was, even in the midst of the battle.

The fat man reached to his belt and pulled out a revolver, which he began firing in the general direction of the storage house. His blind fire was more accurate than it probably would have been had he been able to aim, and chips of wood flew from the edge of the doorway and lodged in the side of Matt's face. The man yelled and rolled away, and Hopper's rifle pumped two slugs into the blinded gunman, knocking him backwards into the dirt. He groaned once, loudly, then lay still.

Jernigan was already lighting the fuse of a second stick of dynamite. He raised up to toss the explosive just as a rifle cracked from the chapel. The slug missed hitting Jernigan seriously, but it grazed his arm enough to throw off his aim. The stick landed almost under the two huge log doors of the front wall of the enclosure, the fuse fizzling.

Then a tremendous blast rendered the door into splinters.

There came a loud yell from the rear of the enclosure, and Matt jerked his head around to discern its origin. It was the white-haired man, astride a large stallion he had taken from the stable in the midst of the confusion of battle. He ran it full speed for the blasted-away doors, then out into the open prairie. He moved so swiftly and unexpectedly that no one even tried to get off a shot at him.

As Matt watched the man disappear out the destroyed doors, he hoped that Melissa had obeyed his instructions and was now safely above on the canyon rim. If not, the mysterious rider might well find her.

As Jernigan hurled a third stick straight into the nearest window of the chapel, Matt fancied that he heard the scream of a girl outside the walls. It chilled him, for there was only one person who it could have come from. Melissa hadn't followed his instructions after all, and now she was caught by the silver-haired rider who had just made such an unexpected escape.

The west wall of the chapel buckled out like a house of cards falling in a gust of wind, and stone and broken mortar showered the courtyard and the side of the storage house. Matt was glad the blast was loud; it drowned out the screams that surely must have burst from the men who died in the blast, killed almost instantly by the tremendous power of the old dynamite. It sickened Matt to think about it.

But even more sickening was the awareness that

Melissa was taken again and in danger once more. Had she only listened to him she would have been safe—but no matter. Now the only thing that mattered was to get her back.

19

i

Melissa was sick—sick to her very soul—as she rode in front of the white-haired man that had bolted from the enclosure moments after that horrible blast that had shattered the doors and knocked her to the ground before she could even attempt to scale the wall and help her rescuers battle the outlaws. She had known that they would be angry at her for such an attempt, but she had no intention of running off to safety as long as there was even a remote chance she could help.

But the blast had stunned her, and even worse, had knocked the old Remington pistol from her hand. She had dug it from her father's saddlebag, aware of his habit of carrying it there as a backup gun, or more of a good luck charm, actually. It had saved his life once on a cattle drive; he had used it to blast the head off a rattler that was springing at his leg. Ever since then he had carried the gun to bring him good luck.

It hadn't worked for Melissa. The crazed, white-headed man had stopped and scooped her up from the ground and sat her on his horse as he bolted from the old monastery, and now they rode together, his head pressing against the side of her face and his breath in her ear. She cried silently, the rushing wind drying her tears almost as quickly as they came.

"Amanda, I knew you would wait for me. I knew you wouldn't leave me. Now we're together, and that's all that matters—that's all that matters. . ."

Who was this man? And who did he think she was? The questions burned in Melissa's mind, antagonizing her, adding to her torment. She did not know what would become of her now, in the hands of this man with no trace of rationality left. It might have been the desire for money that motivated his original capture of her, but that was obviously not what was moving him now. If only she had listened to Matt when he told her to run! It was too late to worry about that now, though, her course had been set, and she would have to take things as they were.

She thought of the three men that had fought, and now maybe died, in the desperate attempt to save her. Perhaps their efforts were to be in vain; perhaps her own carelessness had already undone the good they had accomplished. Waves of self-condemnation swept over her.

The strange man's breath was hot and fast, and from the corner of her eye she saw the smile which contorted his face. Melissa wondered if the men inside the walls had heard her scream, or if they were alive to hear it at all. Even if they were, she doubted that they could come after her, involved as they were in the raging gun battle.

She strained to hear above the pounding horse's hooves and the loud breathing of her captor. It seemed as if the shooting had stopped—what could it mean? One side must have been victorious, and she was doubtful that it was that of her rescuers. She knew that they were outnumbered, and that their ammunition was limited. Her tears flowed faster.

Her sobs were noticed by the white-haired rider behind her in the saddle. "What are you crying for, Amanda? We're together again, and nothing will separate us now. I never dreamed I would see you again—even thought you was dead—but I know now that it ain't so. Don't cry, honey, unless them are tears of joy."

Before them the eastern sky was growing ever brighter. Melissa felt grateful for the light; if by some remote chance someone was left to come after her, they would at least have a clear trail. She twisted her head and looked at the stone wall falling rapidly away behind her. There was no sign of life—only a rising band of dust and smoke which evidenced the blasts that had wracked the structure. She wondered if anyone at all were left alive.

The horse was beginning to tire slightly, and the rider slowed it to a trot. Apparently he felt they were far enough away to give them the edge should anyone pursue them.

The last remnants of revived hope fell away from Melissa's mind. She felt she would never escape this crazed man who thought of her as his lost Amanda, whoever she might be. Images of her father, her mother, Matt, all came flooding into her mind and flashed swiftly across her tear-filled eyes, and at that moment she didn't care if she lived or died.

ii

Hopper was hurt—how badly, no one could tell. Blood was flowing from an ugly wound in the side of his head, created by as large chunk of stone which the final explosion had hurled with cannon-like force at the cowboy. Jernigan and Matt knelt beside him, trying to stop the red flow and perhaps save the life of the wounded man.

Their minds were in a passion of confusion and conflicting priorities. Both were aware of Melissa's recapture—her scream had told them of it—and both were painfully anxious to go after her. But at the same time they could not leave Hopper to die alone and neglected. Jernigan's face was a portrait of violent emotion as he tried to staunch the heavy flow of blood.

"What can I do to help?" Matt asked softly.

The gray-haired rancher glanced up at the young man, then out toward the destroyed door of the monastery. His voice was strangely strained when he said, "Matt, one of us has to go after Melissa. We came all this way just to save her, and we can't let her get away from us at last. I'll stay here and try to help Hopper. You go on—take a horse from their stable over yonder and head out after them. You're a better horseman than me. I'm sorry I can't go with you, but I can't neglect Hopper—not right now."

The man was almost in tears from the frustration and rage aroused by the situation, and Matt felt a powerful sympathy with him. Melissa was the girl he loved, but besides that, she was Ezra Jernigan's daughter. It must be terribly hard for the rancher to stay here while the girl he had raised and loved since her birth was in danger, Matt realized. The man looked suddenly old and tired, and Matt saw that his happiness depended upon what happened out there on the prairie. His future was in Matt's hands, and it seemed an awesome responsibility.

The young man said nothing, but gave Jernigan a look that said far more than words ever could. He grabbed his rifle and took some extra cartridges from Hopper's vest pockets before dashing across the dust-filled, smoky courtyard in the direction of the stable. The sun was bright; the last traces of early-morning dimness were gone.

The light outside made the interior of the stable seem extremely dark as Matt entered. He could hear the stirring of the horses in their stables, so he waited a brief moment for his eyes to grow accustomed to the darkness before he headed for the biggest, strongest-looking stallion he could see.

It was a huge, powerfully built black animal, young and strong. Matt whistled softly and stroked the broad face, giving the beast a clear view of him to keep it from becoming disturbed. It was infinitely important that he be able to thoroughly control his horse, and he didn't want to upset it in any way.

A bridle hung on the opposite wall of the stall, but Matt could find no saddle, and he had no time to search for one. So he grabbed a blanket from a pile in the corner and tossed it over the horse's back. He took the bridle from its peg and fitted it onto the horse's head, adjusting the bit in its mouth.

He leaped up onto the blanket and steered the horse out of the stall. He had done a lot of bareback riding back on the farm in Kansas, so he felt comfortable as he guided the huge animal out of the stall and toward the door.

He ducked his head as the animal loped out of the stable and into the sunlight. It was rested and energetic, just what Matt needed, and he was glad he had not taken the time to run to where his own horse was tethered in the aspen stand west of the monastery. This animal was far superior to his horse, and no doubt it would narrow the distance between Matt and his quarry very rapidly. He dug his heels into the animal's loins, and it snorted and bolted toward the open gate of the front wall.

Jernigan's voice called out an encouraging word as Matt darted out onto the prairie. His eyes scanned the earth, looking for signs of a trail. He had no luck; his horse was moving too fast. Reluctantly he slowed it down, then picked up the trail. He nudged the horse again, speeding eastward.

They had a jump on him, Matt knew, but not a large one. It had only been minutes before that the white-haired man had bolted from the enclosure, so he and Melissa could not be too far ahead. Before Matt was a rise, illuminated from the bright sun. Had the situation been different, he would no doubt noticed the incredible beauty of the Colorado countryside—the rolling, rounded hills, green with summer grass and still glistening with the remnants of the morning dew, and the peaks visible across his shoulder, dim in the distance and snowcapped.

But Matt did not see it. All that existed for him was the fresh trail before him and the purpose of the chase. As he topped the sloping rise, he glanced up. There before him, crossing the next slope, was the rider, Melissa before him in the saddle. He was moving in a trot, apparently unaware of his pursuer. Matt encouraged his horse onward, hoping to lessen the distance between himself and his quarry before he was spotted by the white-haired rider.

Matt's powerful stallion covered the distance in a short time, hardly puffing from the exertion. It was an amazingly powerful and fleet animal, well-adapted for running.

As Matt topped the rise upon which Melissa and her captor had been moments before, he heard the crack of a pistol and the zinging of a bullet ahead of him, bolting around a large, rounded knoll of rock that jutted up promontory-like in the midst of the plain.

Matt's mind worked quickly, setting up the only course of action possible. He guided his hard-running horse straight for the knoll, hoping to reach it before his enemey rounded the other side and got off another shot at him. The speed of his black stallion was incredible, closing the distance with remarkable swiftness.

The knoll sloped up on the westward side, facing Matt, while the eastern edge was a sheer drop of about twenty feet. The big rock was like a huge wedge laying flat on the plain, its slope extending toward Matt like a ramp. At the opposite end of that wedge was the rider and Melissa. It was not a comfortable feeling, knowing that at any second the man could appear on either side of the knoll, blasting Matt from his saddle before he could evade the shot.

Matt had one thing going for him—the speed of his horse. He guessed that the man would time his attack based on his estimation of the time it would take an average horse to bring its rider within pistol range. But Matt's horse was no average animal, and what was more, he had no intention of riding around either side of that knoll to certain death. As he approached the base of the slope long before the adversary expected him, he guided his horse straight up the slope, heading for the top.

When he reached it, he quickly dismounted, tethering his horse to a scrubby bush and crawling on his stomach to the edge of the bluff. He looked carefully over, and as he expected, saw the rider dismounted, his back hugging the slope and his pistol drawn, obviously waiting for Matt to come barrelling around the side of the knoll.

Matt wasted no time. He jumped quietly up and loosened his horse, leading it quickly down the slope again. When he reached the base, he slapped it hard on the thigh and steered it in the direction the white-haired man obviously was expecting. The riderless animal snorted fiercely and loped off at a fast trot.

Matt ran full-steam up the slope again, coming to the top just as the horse rounded the back. The waiting man turned quickly and fired two quick shots at the animal, sending lead whizzing across where Matt would have been had he been seated on it. Matt could hear Melissa's scream as the shots were fired, and at that moment he jumped.

He landed full-force upon the back of the white-haired man, knocking him to the earth. He could hear the gasps and cries of Melissa as he began pummelling the man, letting his blows fall where they would. He was grateful for one thing: He had knocked the pistol from the man's grasp when he struck him from above.

Matt rained blows upon the man's kidneys, but the older man twisted hard, like a dog trying to dislodge a cat from its back. Matt was forced off, and he rolled quickly, standing and wheeling around to face his enemey eye-to-eye for the first time.

Or so he thought. Before he even got to his feet all the way, the man's rock-hard first caught him squarely on the jaw and sent him flying onto his back. Before he could rise a sharp boot struck him again and again, sending lightning-flashes of pain through his body.

The older man threw himself on top of the young man, his fists beating almost thythmically upon his victim's face. He straddled Matt's chest, punctuating every blow with a curse. Matt knew he would quickly lose consciousness if this continued. So he stretched out his arms beside him and brought them up sharply, palms flat, and landed them hard upon the old man's ears.

He cried out in pain and rolled off Matt, and Matt saw the glitter of a knife as it fell to the earth. His tactic had come just in time—a second later and the man would have stabbed him.

Matt rushed the man, throwing himself at him with every intent of knocking him to the earth. To his surprise, the old man's boot caught him in the abdomen and sent him flying. Matt rolled when he hit, and spun around to face his foe.

He looked into the face of Will Monroe. Or rather, a grotesque parody of that face, a twisted and pain-filled travesty of the man Matt had known, now aged beyond his years and obviously devoid of his reason.

As unbelievable as it was, Matt knew instantaneously and beyond a doubt that it was Monroe—the steel-gray eyes were unmistakeable. But yet those same eyes had a strange, blank look to them, something that looked deranged. The sharp rationality and instinctive brilliance that had shown so clearly in the man's face six years before was gone now, entirely gone. And he looked older—ever so much older. Something had happened that had rendered him only a pitiful shell of his former self.

But as the panting old man stared in confusion at the younger man before him, there came into his eyes for a moment something like recognition. He opened his mouth slightly, and his piercing gray eyes regained a little of the clearness that Matt had first noticed in the dim light of the Briar Creek jail six years before.

"Matt?" The voice that sounded the name was so weak, so quivering and unsure that Matt could scarcely make it out.

Matt found his throat strangely constricted, and it was long moments before he could force his voice out.

"Yes, Will, it's me—Matt. I never thought—I never thought I would see you again, especially not like—like this." He paused, then added softly, "What's happened to you, Will?"

Tears suddenly flooded the gray eyes, and the

snowy head dropped its gaze from Matt's face. "Fever, Matt. About three years back. I was sick—so sick! I almost didn't live through it. And it changed me. . .changed me like you can see." He looked up again, and spoke more vigorously, like a man whose only outlet for misery was words. "It turned my hair white, made me older than I am. And ever since then, it's been hard. . .so hard. . .for me to think. It's as if the world is in a haze, and I just can't think right. . .can't think right. . ."

Already Matt could see the faint glimmer of rationality that had arisen in the man's eyes begin to fade. His brief trip into the world of reality was over. He looked at Matt as a different person than he was only a moment before.

"But things are gonna be good for me again, 'cause my Amanda's come back! I thought I'd lost her years before—thought she had died back in Idaho—but here she is! And I'm never gonna let her go away again. . .no. . .she's mine now. . . forever. God—how I love her!"

He gazed strangely at Matt then. "But you. . . you want to take her from me!" And before Matt could shake himself out of his daze enough to realize what was happening, Monroe had scooped up the pistol which he had lost when the fight began. And it was aimed straight at Matt's head.

"Will—think a minute! I'm Matt. You know me! Don't you remember all that we went through together? I'm your friend, Will, your friend!"

It was obvious that his words were having no effect. A palsied thumb slowly cocked back the hammer of the revolver and a trembling arm raised the gun in a shaky though deadly accurate aim.

177

And it was just before Monroe's finger began to squeeze down on the trigger that Melissa moved.

She thrust herself directly in front of the outlaw, between him and her lover. And with determination and surprising strength in her voice she spoke.

"You'll have to kill me first."

The pain that showed in Monroe's face was so real and horrible that it drove like a dagger through Matt's heart. He knew full well that the old outlaw was ready to kill him, yet he could feel no anger—only pity.

The hand shook even more violently and the gun lowered.

"Amanda?" Then more loudly, "Amanda—God, no! Amanda!"

The scream that issued from the throat of the man sent a horrible chill through Matt. It was hard, almost impossible, to believe that this was the same man who he had loved so dearly only a few years before, a man who now had almost ceased to be a human, and who lived in the long-forgotten past instead of the present.

Matt had to turn away when the old man lifted the gun to his own head. He couldn't look when the bullet tore through the man's brain, destroying what little had been left by the ravaging fever years before. Melissa screamed in unison with the roar of the gun, then there was silence, total and complete.

Will Monroe was dead by his own hand. There was something unfair about it, something so unjust that it sickened Matt even more than the bloody corpse itself. He pulled Melissa to him and turned his back on the horrible scene.

There was nothing but the brilliant light of the Colorado sun, the noise of the wind, and the muffled sounds of weeping as Matt hugged Melissa to him and cried unashamedly. Not since the death of his father had he cried, but now the tears flowed freely.

20

It was a long time before the couple ceased clinging to each other. Matt wept, for his loss was great, and Melissa cried also. But hers were tears of joy at her release from a man so insane she feared he would kill her. Matt removed his shirt and placed it over the mangled and pitiful head of the man who years ago had been his friend, but who had died his enemy. He placed his arm around Melissa and the two strode off toward the two stallions that were grazing placidly in the grassland beyond the knoll.

"Matt"—her voice was soft and gentle—"you knew him, didn't you?" It was more of a statement than a question.

Matt didn't answer immediately. That was one part of his life that he had never planned on sharing with her. He felt that the mistakes of the past were better left dead and unrevived. It was strange how times which he thought buried in the distant past had arisen to meet him in the present! Still, Melissa had a right to know, he realized, especially after all she had been through.

Matt struggled for the right words. How could

he tell her of his relationship with Will Monroe without revealing too much? And just how much did she need to know?

"It was several years ago, back in my old home in Kansas," he said at length. "I got myself into some trouble, and he got me out of it. I—I really don't want to say much more than that."

He stopped and turned toward the weary, beautiful girl, grasping her shoulders in his hands and looking deep into her brown eyes.

"He wasn't always like he was when you saw him. You heard him say himself that his mind was gone, and anyway, I guess I could tell that just from looking at him." He paused, swallowed hard to clear the mountain forming in his throat, then quietly said, "There was a time when he was a good man, Melissa—a good man."

That was all he could find to say.

Melissa's eyes had never been so beautiful as they were that morning in the clear Colorado sunlight. She looked deeply into Matt's face, then pulled him to her and kissed him. He wrapped his arms around her and crushed her to him, feeling the love flow between them. He loved her dearly, even more dearly than he had imagined.

Melissa's lips parted from his and she looked at him again, her hand stroking his tousled hair. "I believe you, Matt. There's no need for you to say anything else. I'm not interested in your past, nor in who that man was. All I care about is us—right now. That's what matters."

At that moment Matt found the strength to say what he had longed to say for so long. He gazed at her brown, shining eyes, glistening like the dew-covered grass around them, and asked, "Melissa, could you ever consider—consider marrying some-one like me?'' It was like a heavy load off his shoulders when he spoke the words.

And his heart nearly leaped from his chest in jubilation when she smiled and responded, not in words, but in a firm, sincere nod of her lovely head. Again he pulled her to him, and again he kissed her, long and hard.

When the two rode up to the old monastery again they found Jernigan standing beside Hopper, who was seated on the ground with his back against the stone wall. In spite of the wounded cowboy's deeply bronzed skin his face looked weak and pale—but he was alive, his head bandaged with his bandana. Matt and Melissa greeted the men in a long ritual of hugs and handshakes. Melissa was weeping in ecstasy and relief.

Jernigan hugged his daughter close for a long time before he spoke anything more than muffled words of joy at her safe return. It was evident that he had been far more tense and worried than he previously allowed himself to show. His over-whelming relief at his daughter's safety was apparent in his clumsy, crushing hug and the happiness which shone in his rugged face. No one spoke—it seemed far too sacred a moment.

At length the rancher looked at Matt. ''I heard shootin'. Did you kill him?''

Matt glanced hurriedly at Melissa. Her gaze told him that she would say nothing of what had occurred beyond what he chose to tell. It was up to Matt to reveal as much or as little as he wanted of the tragic drama which had taken place beyond the knoll.

Into his mind for a moment came the memory of Will Monroe's face in the coal oil light of the Briar Creek jail, and in the darkness on the roof where they had lay the night they made their escape. He saw again the troubled expression on Monroe's face when Matt had awaked from his stupor in old Jimmy's shed. He remembered the distant form of the outlaw as he rode across the Kansas grasslands when they had parted company six years before.

It seemed like minutes to Matt, but all those memories flitted across his memory for only the briefest fraction of an instant. He looked into Jernigan's face.

"Yes sir, I killed him."

Melissa said nothing, but only looked at her lover, the light in her gaze undimmed.

Jernigan sighed. "It's over, then. You have no idea who this gang was, Matt? Hopper and me didnt't know any of 'em."

Matt's eyes saddened imperceptibly for only a moment. "No, sir, Mr. Jernigan. It was nobody I knew." He looked at the ground. "Nobody at all."

A sudden chuckle burst from Hopper. "Well, our old friend is about gone, I see!" Matt looked at the cowboy, then followed his gaze out to where the tiny distant form of a horseman disappeared over a hill.

"Who's that, Pa?" Melissa asked.

"Him? Oh, just a sentry who we surprised a little earlier. We had no use for him, so we let him go—wearing only his longjohns, of course!"

Then they all laughed loud and hard, Hopper wincing as every spasm of mirth shot pain through his aching head. It felt good to Matt to laugh again.

Jernigan spoke. "Hopper, you think you're up to ridin' just yet?"

The cowboy grinned. "Ain't nothin' that could keep me from it, Ezra."

"Then let's go home."

From every throat but one came a burst of assent to the proposition. Matt spoke quietly. "You all go on ahead. Melissa can ride my horse. I'll take this stallion. I'll catch up to you on the trail."

Jernigan sensed that inquiry into Matt's strange action would be inappropriate right then, so after a short pause he nodded quietly at the man before him.

"All right, Matt. You do whatever you need to."

Several minutes later Matt stood alone before the monastery, watching his friends disappear into the aspen stand on the first leg of the homeward journey. His face was powerful in its expression, though touched slightly with a trace of sorrow. He waited until he could no longer see any trace of his partners before he moved.

Then he turned and walked through the shattered doors of the Beggar's Gulch monastery to look for a shovel.

WINTER SHADOWS

Will Henry

From the very beginning of his long and illustrious career, Will Henry wrote from the Native American viewpoint with authenticity and compassion. This volume collects two of his finest short novels, each focused on the American Indian. The title novel finds a band of Mandan Indians facing the harshest winter in their history, while having to deal with an unscrupulous medicine man. *Lapwai Winter* is set in Northeastern Oregon at the time of Chief Joseph of the Nez Perce. A treaty is violated, the territorial rights of the tribe are revoked . . . and the threat of war hangs ominously in the air.

THE LEGEND
OF THE
MOUNTAIN
Will Henry

Everything Will Henry wrote was infused with historical accuracy, filled with adventure, and peopled with human, believable characters. In this collection of novellas, Will Henry turns his storyteller's gaze toward the American Indian. "The Rescue of Chuana" follows the dangerous attempt by the Apache Kid to rescue his beloved from the Indian School in New Mexico Territory. "The Friendship of Red Fox" is the tale of a small band of Oglala Sioux who have escaped from the Pine Ridge Reservation to join up with Sitting Bull. And in "The Legend of Sotoju Mountain" an old woman and a young brave must find and defeat the giant black grizzly known to their people as Mato Sapa.

WILL COOK

THE DEVIL'S ROUNDUP

Will Cook has long been regarded as one of the finest writers of the Western's Golden Age. These five short novels, among Cook's best, are all set in Hondo, Texas, and the surrounding ranching community, and take place over a period of twenty years. Many of the same characters appear throughout as they age, marry, have children and fight to survive in a wild and violent land. This thrilling saga reveals an entire frontier community's growth through moments filled with excitement, drama and highly memorable characters.

STEPHEN OVERHOLSER

FIRE IN THE RAINBOW

Red Rock County, Colorado has a population of 999 people. The beef population, however, is mysteriously decreasing as various local ranches begin reporting missing or stolen cattle. When it's discovered that cattle with doctored brands are being sold across the Colorado border in New Mexico Territory, it falls to Deputy Sheriff Cale Parker to investigate. As Cale starts to dig deeper into the disappearances, he quickly learns that there are people in the county who would like very much to see the human population decrease by one. Namely, one nosy deputy!

TWO TONS OF GOLD

TODHUNTER BALLARD

The Bank of California in the 1860s is a powerful company that pays its mine workers very little and will not tolerate strikes, sending in vicious strikebreakers to beat down any opposition. When Major Mark Dorne's father is murdered by strikebreakers, he begins a one-man war against the bank, always leaving behind his calling card—a small silver coin. Now the Major is ready for his most daring attack yet, the theft of five million dollars in gold coins from the Bank of California, from under the noses of the Wells Fargo guards. But his enemies are aware of his plans and have devised a foolproof plan to stop this war once and for all!

MAX BRAND®

THE PERIL TREK

Max Brand has never been equaled for his tales of the Old West, tales that combine historical accuracy, grand adventure and humanity. This exciting trio of novellas includes the title story, Brand's final episode in the thrilling saga of Reata, one of his most popular characters. Reata has finally freed himself from master criminal Pop Dickerman, but then he meets Bob Clare, a man living under the constant threat of death. Clare enlists Reata's aid, but to help him Reata has to once again confront Dickerman, and this time there's no telling what might happen.

Dorchester Publishing Co., Inc.
P.O. Box 6640
Wayne, PA 19087-8640
_____5267-9
$5.50 US/$7.50 CAN

Please add $2.50 for shipping and handling for the first book and $.75 for each additional book. NY and PA residents, add appropriate sales tax. No cash, stamps, or CODs. Canadian orders require $2.00 for shipping and handling and must be paid in U.S. dollars. Prices and availability subject to change. **Payment must accompany all orders.**

Name: _____

Address: _____

City: _____ State: _____ Zip: _____

E-mail: _____

I have enclosed $_____ in payment for the checked book(s).

For more information on these books, check out our website at www.dorchesterpub.com.
_____ *Please send me a free catalog.*

MEN BEYOND THE LAW

These three short novels showcase Max Brand doing what he does best: exploring the wild, often dangerous life beyond the constraints of cities, beyond the reach of civilization . . . beyond the law. Whether he's a desperate man fleeing the tragic results of a gunfight, an innocent young man who stumbles onto the loot from a bank robbery, or the gentle giant named Bull Hunter—one of Brand's most famous characters—each protagonist is out on his own, facing two unknown frontiers: the Wild West . . . and his own future.

___4873-6 $4.50 US/$5.50 CAN

Dorchester Publishing Co., Inc.
P.O. Box 6640
Wayne, PA 19087-8640

Please add $2.50 for shipping and handling for the first book and $.75 for each book thereafter. NY, NYC, and PA residents, please add appropriate sales tax. No cash, stamps, or C.O.D.s. All orders shipped within 6 weeks via postal service book rate. Canadian orders require $2.50 extra postage and must be paid in U.S. dollars through a U.S. banking facility.

Name_____
Address_____
City_____State_____Zip_____
I have enclosed $_____ in payment for the checked book(s).
Payment __must__ accompany all orders. ☐ Please send a free catalog.
     CHECK OUT OUR WEBSITE! www.dorchesterpub.com